WHERE
SHE
BELONGS

Pamela Harstad

ISBN: 9798667111245

DEDICATION

This book is dedicated to the many who struggle
for acceptance and finding their true pathway in life.

Also by
Pamela Harstad

ERIN'S MISSION

HEALING JOURNEY

THEIR GREEK KEY

AS WE FORGIVE THOSE

ACKNOWLEDGMENTS

Many people and issues over a period of years have helped contribute to the creation of this book, especially the people of Hawaii from numerous visits there. In addition, I want to thank the writers and editors, and my critique partner for their valuable input and suggestions. Thanks to Russell Photography of Cedar Falls, Iowa for providing the author photo. And lastly, thanks to friends and family who encourage and support me in my writing endeavors.

CHAPTER ONE

Would it work for her? Leilani Hudson spotted
the dwelling right outside the town of Lahaina, Maui. An
old-style green and white plantation house with a rusty,
tin roof. Tears stung her eyes as she pulled into the drive.
No vandalism. No evictions here.

Thankful for this inheritance when she had
nowhere to live, could she afford the expenses of a
house?

Inside, she glanced around the small, one
bedroom abode. A real home. So what if the house was
rundown, moldy and out of date? But now to make it
feasible to stay.

Outside, trade winds tousled her hair as she
locked the house. Her mending business in Kahului
would entail a forty-five minute drive from Lahaina. It
made sense to work in Lahaina given the long drive to
Kahului, the cost of gas, her ancient car and meager
earnings. But Lahaina was a much smaller community

near tourists and resorts. Without enough customers, there'd be less work for her here. But she adored this house. Could it be more perfect?

She stepped across the grass littered with plumeria blossoms toward her car.

"Well, well. Look who's come out to greet me."

The familiar, cynical voice jolted Lei to an abrupt stop. Acid churned its way into her throat. "Eric." With arms crossed and adrenaline gushing through her veins, she hated the way her voice trembled. "Why are you here?"

He moved closer, invading her space. "Can't an old friend wish you well on your move, evidently to this dump?"

Old friend? After the way he'd treated her? Breathing proved difficult, but she managed to spit it out. "I'm leaving now."

He threw his head back, and his chin jutted out. "Why? I just got here."

"I'm ready to go. What do you want, anyway?" She quivered inside, but managed to remain motionless enough to keep a strong stance.

"Why, nothing. Since you didn't tell me you were leaving, I had to do all the work to find you myself." He kicked hard at a few of the plumeria blooms in the grass and dug into the red soil.

Lei stepped to one side of the yard to bypass him and walked toward the car.

Eric blocked her path. "Course, you're easy to track. Nothing to following you."

Her leg muscles tightened, ready to sprint if necessary. Why wouldn't he leave her alone? "I don't try to hide where I go." Could he hear the hitch in her voice?

"Remember, I can find you whenever I want, if I want."

Every muscle tensed as her pulse rose at an alarming rate. Chin lifted high, she was so done with this. "So? Is this how you want to spend your time, following me around? Pathetic. You need to get a life." She balled her hands into tight fists to keep them from shaking.

"Oh, but I do have one." He snorted.

The pitch of her voice increased. "Then go live it and leave me alone. Do you want me to get a restraining order? I will if you keep bothering me."

Eric chuckled. "Oh, please. You're making a big deal out of nothing. So typical of you. And besides, everyone knows those things don't work."

Lei wanted to scream in his face but wouldn't give him the satisfaction. He'd take it as weakness and an opportunity to upset her.

The hibiscus bushes behind her rustled. She turned and saw a man. Her stomach churned. Who was he? Did Eric bring someone with him?

He stepped out past the bushes into the yard and faced Lei. "Hi. I'm your new neighbor, Jess Park. I recently moved here from the mainland and will start security work at the Hawaiian Hotel. Nice to meet you."

The tall, good-looking man mesmerized her for a moment. Was it his light brown, wavy hair tousled by the wind, or the sea-green eyes which caught her gaze? And what a polite manner after Eric's harsh tone.

Eric sauntered forward and greeted the newcomer, his chest thrust out. "How sweet. I'm Eric. For the record, I do my own security and investigation. And I'm good at it."

Heat filled her cheeks from the semi-veiled threat. "Please ignore those comments." She extended her hand toward Jess and suspected he'd overheard the prior conversation with Eric. "Leilani Hudson. People call me Lei. I'm from Maui, but new to this side of the island."

Eric glowered.

Jess pressed his lips into a tight line, but then the corners twitched upward.

Good. She liked him. "I'll be moving in soon." Her upper lip curled when she glared at Eric. "Alone."

Her mind raced. In one day she'd viewed her new home, faced employment concerns, dealt with an encounter from Eric and met a man who captivated her like no one else.

CHAPTER TWO

Jess stood his ground near the hibiscus bushes and waited for Eric's next move. The guy had arrogant and control down to a fine art.

The silence drew out, but Eric shifted from one foot to the other. Body language told the truth every time.

Arms loose by his side, posture erect, feet shoulder's width apart, Jess waited for the other man to break. No way would he leave Lei here to fend for herself. And he couldn't invite her over until Eric left, not without escalating the mounting animosity. He had suspicions about the guy. Who knew what someone like Eric was capable of doing?

"I'll be seeing you around real soon." Eric leaned toward Lei like he wanted to kiss her.

Her head recoiled. She made a choking noise in her throat and turned away from him.

Eric laughed as he marched off toward his car.

Stepping farther into Lei's yard, Jess faced her. "Sorry. I didn't mean to interfere, but the investigator in me sometimes takes over."

"Not at all. Thank you. Eric talks big, but he's physically harmless."

Hands on his hips, he drew in a breath. Lei and all women deserved better. "Nevertheless, it's abusive and harassment."

"Yeah, but I don't pay him much mind anymore. He kind of touched a raw nerve today, however. I met him a while back, found out what kind of person he was and let him loose. Or so I thought. Unfortunately, he pops up every once in a while. I'm sure as soon as he finds someone else he'll be gone for good."

What an extraordinary woman. She could take care of herself, yet something vulnerable came through those gorgeous brown eyes while Eric spoke to her.

Should he ask her now? He folded his hands to keep them at rest. "Would you like to come over for a glass of iced tea?"

Lei hesitated, looked in the direction of Eric's car and then back at Jess. "I shouldn't."

"No problem." He wouldn't push her after the tension with Eric. "I understand."

She tilted her head and pursed her lips. "Okay. Maybe for a few minutes."

A smile stretched his mouth wide. He guided her from her yard through the widest opening in the red, hibiscus bushes and into his house. Lei's glance took in the kitchen and living area, approval written on her face.

"Nice place, Jess. It's laid out similar to my house."

Taking the iced tea from the refrigerator, he grabbed two glasses from the cupboard and poured the tea. "It's okay for now. I'm not staying here too long. Only until things work out for me the way I've planned for my future."

An extended arm toward the kitchen table and chairs sent her moving in the direction to take a seat.

"Plans are good. I wish I could have the same confidence, but mine don't often work for me. Yet moving into the house next door was a great surprise. I'm thrilled to have it. And a new neighbor, too." She studied his face for several seconds. "Jess, what brought you to Lahaina?"

Jess set the glasses on the kitchen table, condensation forming on the outside of the tumblers and sat across from her. "It's my hope to land a job as a special investigator on Oahu in time and kick-start my career. I was born on Oahu, but I've been away for a long time. In the meantime, I snagged a temporary job at the hotel, so it's why I came to Maui. What about you?"

She sipped the tea. "The house is an inheritance from my *tutu's* spouse, my grandmother's husband who passed away. His great-nephew and my two siblings received an equal amount of cash, but thankfully I received the house since I needed a place to live. I have a seamstress mending business in Kahului, but it's too expensive for me to drive back and forth daily. Unfortunately, most of my clients are there, so I'm not sure what I'll do for gathering enough customers here and making a living. Hopefully something with sewing, but we'll see. Maybe I'll advertise and in the meantime sew some items needed for the house."

Jess poured himself more tea. "If you're planning on making some stuff for your plantation house, would you consider doing the same for me? I'm not into the décor scene at all, but even I can tell this place needs warming up. I mean it's nice, but it's not homey."

"Sure. Let me know what you need."

His fingers made paths through the moisture on the glass. "Lots. I'll want a couple tablecloths to start. Later on maybe some throw pillows. I'll pay you whatever you charge. I don't know about prices either."

With a clink of her glass against his, she nodded. "It's a deal. It may take me a while until I get settled. But it also depends on whether I get any work. Who knows? You might be my one and only client if there isn't much opportunity for me around here."

He tapped his index finger over his lips as a thought wormed its way into his mind. "I have an idea. Once you're settled, you should come with me to the Hawaiian Hotel sometime when I have a day off. They have all kinds of Hawaiian made crafts for sale from vendors. If you can make tablecloths and throw pillows, you could sell them there. Plus, they have an awesome pastor who preaches on the weekends. I met him before I took the job and he has lived here most of his life. He might also have resources for you."

A wide smile adorned her beautiful face. Something about her drew him in and made him want to know more about her. Everything. But he'd respect her boundaries. Besides, he kept issues close to his heart as well, things he shared with no one else.

"Sounds good. I'll think about it." She glanced at the computer screen on the table. "I couldn't help but notice you have a DNA site."

"Yeah, I'm definitely into it. I like genealogy, but the DNA is especially interesting and great if someone wants to find you." He paused. "Or if you want to find someone."

She tossed her gorgeous, black hair behind her shoulders. "Hmm. I've never had much of an interest. I'm more about looking forward in life these days. Sometimes it's difficult for me to look back."

Lei had no idea how much he related to those words. He snapped his fingers. "Maybe you've got something there. I do look to my future, but often look back. Since I'm in laid-back Hawaii now, I should make a point of taking each day as it comes. Live in the moment and enjoy my surroundings."

She pushed her empty glass toward his and stood. "Yeah. It's rather difficult for me at times, but I think there's a reason for everything in our lives and God's will for us in each day if we look for it. Not saying it's easy, of course."

He couldn't hold back a smile. "With you moving in next door to me, I'm sure it'll hold true. You've given me something to think about before you even take up residence here."

She grinned as a blush showed on her cheeks. "I should get going."

With a few, short steps he followed her to the door. "Let me know if I can do anything to help with the move. I was glad to see someone come through the property the other day and hoped for a new neighbor to arrive. It's way too quiet around here. And now you're here. Welcome."

She gazed up at him, eyes wide open. "It wasn't Eric, was it?"

A quick frown revealed he'd upset her. Maybe Eric's presence bothered her more than she realized. "No, definitely not. I only saw the man for a few seconds from the back, but his hair was a lighter color and shorter than Eric's. I thought maybe it was the owner, but I didn't see him or anyone else go inside the place. He didn't bother anything. I would've notified the police if he had. It was broad daylight. Maybe someone passing through was all. I didn't mean to worry you."

"Good to know. Thanks, Jess."

He extended his arm. "Would you like me to walk you to your car?"

"No. Thanks for the tea."

The sway of her hips as she walked across the lawn held him fixated until she disappeared through the hibiscus bushes.

This strong willed, beautiful woman intrigued him. She needed to build her business here in Lahaina, but also had an annoying, unwanted man bothering her. His gut told him Eric probably wouldn't give up with his harassment right away. He could make life difficult for her.

Jess scratched his chin and headed back inside, plagued by the strangest urge to gather her into his arms and protect her in the future. Not happening. He'd proceed with care where she was concerned. He wouldn't let impulses spoil a relationship.

He was human, had sinned, asked forgiveness for his past and now walked in God's path as best he could.

Lei said she'd rather look forward in life, something he would work on for himself. Therefore, no further searching for today. Jess heaved out a sigh and closed the laptop.

*

Early the next morning, Jess Park glanced out the open, kitchen screen window. A pink plumeria tree dropped a few flowers which twirled like pinwheels onto the shiny, dew-soaked grass. The rich, fragrant scent filled his nostrils and eased the ache in his heart. Ah, this was Maui, a much-needed change from the mainland. Now with a chance to start his life over, Hawaii should prove a great opportunity for his career goals, too.

A glance around the kitchen and living area of the small cottage made him grin. Close to his new job, he'd been able to rent it by the month so he could leave in a hurry if his dream job became available on Oahu.

Jess unlocked the door, leaving it open to get some breeze through the screen door. In the meantime, Lei would help him make the place his own. Jess couldn't wait until she moved in next door. Not planning on a relationship, it might happen all the same. He couldn't get the woman out of his mind.

Later he'd drive to the Hawaiian Hotel for his temporary security guard orientation, but for now he stepped out into the yard and basked in the warm, Hawaiian summer sun.

A small, tanned woman with gray hair walked into the yard holding a weaved basket.

"Aloha. I'm Mrs. Chen, next door neighbor." She extended her hand. "Nice to meet you."

Jess took her tiny hand in his and gave it a pump. "Jess Park. Pleasure's mine. I appreciate friendly neighbors."

"Taro bread for you. Baked fresh." Mrs. Chen extended the container toward him. "Some people don't like the purple color, but it tastes the same."

The morning sunlight dazzled through the plumeria branches as Jess grabbed the edge of the basket and peeked inside of it. What a treat. "I haven't had this bread since I was a boy when I lived on Oahu. My dad was stationed at Hickam Air Force base for several years after I was born there."

A smile crept through her wrinkled face. "For goodness' sake. A local boy."

"Yes, ma'am." He removed the sack of rolls.

Mrs. Chen stared up at him with a sparkle in her eyes. "Welcome. Ah, so you know, things mostly quiet around here, but I keep watch when I'm not at my daughter's place."

Nice to know Lei would have an observant neighbor while he worked, in case Eric showed again. "Glad to have a good neighborhood watch." He wiped his brow. "Did you know someone is moving in next to me?"

The old woman lifted her chin. "I noticed someone. A man."

Had Mrs. Chen seen or heard Eric last night? Or maybe the man Jess spied on Lei's property the day before he met her? He wouldn't ask, having only met Mrs. Chen. This wasn't an interrogation, for heaven's sake. "A young lady is moving in soon."

Her head tipped back. "Oh, good. We'll have a full neighborhood again soon."

"I'll be working at the Hawaiian Hotel in security. If there's ever anything I can do for you, let me know."

Her index finger touched parted lips. "Now if trouble ever comes, I know who to call. *Mahalo*."

"You certainly do. And thank you, too, for the visit and the taro bread. I can't wait to taste it."

Back at the kitchen table he opened his laptop. The keys clicked as he checked on the jobsite for the criminal investigation position he waited for on Oahu. No openings yet, of course. Living in Hawaii, he'd have the advantage to move sooner than most others would from the mainland. If he got the job, he'd have the money he needed to continue his search later on, once established in his career.

Jess grabbed a taro roll and poured himself a glass of milk from the small fridge next to the sink. Returning to the table, he bit into the soft, roll and washed it down with a sip of the cold milk. A moan escaped. So good. The delicious, fresh bread brought back warm memories of his childhood in the islands. Yes, he'd made the right decision moving here without a doubt. He looked forward to his current job and getting to know Lei.

After finishing the roll and milk, Jess settled in front of his laptop. Quick strokes brought up the DNA website where he'd posted his report. No close matches as usual, but one day maybe someone would give him a lead. In the meantime, he'd do what he did best. Persevere. Continue the proverbial search for the needle in the haystack, but only now and then. Yes, he'd made the break and moved away, but he had a right and responsibility for this search, didn't he?

With a sigh, he closed the laptop and grabbed the car keys from the hook on the wall. Jess drew in a breath and stared at the worn-out, vinyl floor.

Tomorrow she'd turn seven years old.

CHAPTER THREE

Lei stacked the bolts of fabric on the kitchen table she'd brought along when she'd moved into the plantation house last week. Jess would arrive home from work any moment now and she couldn't wait for him to choose the colors he wanted.

With the individual swatches arranged, she glanced around the living room area at the few pictures she'd hung. The slipcovers she'd made for the worn-out chairs made it feel more like home, too. The house gave her joy but required plenty of responsibility to keep it running. A challenge worth working for provided she could find enough employment. Jess kicked off her first big order.

A rap on the screen door rattled it. "Aloha."

Her mouth fell open. "Kimo. What a surprise to see my brother here." She unlatched the screen door. Tall and lanky, he looked so much like their father had, except Kimo had black hair and brown eyes like their Hawaiian mother.

"I've wanted to explore the island again, so I thought I'd drop by along the way. I'm taking a drive around, seeing what's changed since I left for foster care on Oahu." He peered into the house.

"Please come in." She extended her arm toward the living room. He'd missed Maui. Understandable. It made her grateful she and her sister, Malia didn't have to leave the island during their foster care. "Have a seat."

Kimo sat on the sofa. "So this is the gifted house." He continued gazing around, his lips slightly parted. "Not the Taj Mahal, but decent enough."

Lei sat in the chair opposite from him. "Yeah." She pointed. "There's one bedroom and the bath besides this kitchen and living area. You're welcome to look at them if you like."

"Thanks. Maybe on my way out. I've heard some of these old places can have relics, like ancient Hawaiian artifacts and stuff. You better look around. Never know."

Her posture stiffened. The comment struck her as odd coming from a teenager. Who gave him such an idea? "I've had a chance to look through the house. Not much here besides the old pieces of furniture and a few odds and ends." Time to change the subject. "Where's Elle?"

He stretched back in the chair and placed his hands behind his head. "Doing her own thing. We're not attached to each other every waking moment."

"Of course not." A good thing in her opinion. They were both so young. But Malia claimed Elle worshiped him.

"Besides, I wanted to check out some of the places we used to go when we were kids. I need to do it by myself."

She moved forward, understanding Kimo's loss of their parents and home. "Having to go to Oahu made it even worse for you. I'm really sorry." Her voice shook and she blinked back tears.

15

"You know Tutu didn't have a husband or the means at the time to take us in or she would have."

His head tilted to the side. "Yeah, I know. I get it. The worst was never really belonging in the foster homes, no matter how nice the families were."

"It's how it was for me, too. I had decent families to live with and a roof over my head, but deep inside I didn't belong." Desperate to fit in, she'd jumped into a relationship with Eric and ended up worse off, but wouldn't share it with Kimo. He had his own issues.

He moved forward toward the edge of the sofa. "Know what? I don't want to belong anywhere or to anyone now, the more I think about it. I'm starting to enjoy my freedom."

"Will you start college when you go back to Oahu, since we have our inheritance now?" She wrung her hands and waited for his answer.

Kimo sat upright. "Who says I'm going back to Oahu?"

Eyes wide, her jaw dropped. "No one. I assumed you would go back. You'd talked about a scholarship and college there."

"Right now, I'm enjoying riding around Maui." Kimo pointed toward the living room window facing the driveway.

A glance out the window showed a new, shiny, red vehicle. A make of car not recognizable to her, but with an expensive look to it. Her voice lilted upward. "You bought a car with your inheritance?"

"Yup. Cool, isn't it?" With a quick grin, his chin lifted, pride written all over him.

Her tone became hushed. "Beautiful." If she mentioned the extravagance of it, he'd bolt.

"I'll bring Elle around another day."

"Please do. I'd like to get to know her better." Lei pressed her palms together and tried to hide her surprise about the car.

Kimo rose, walked by the bedroom and then the bath. "Hmm. Not bad." He moved near the door. "Guess I'll take off."

Her body heavy, Lei rubbed the back of her neck and joined him by the kitchen door. He wouldn't return to Oahu and attend college. "I'm glad you came. Do you have any other plans for your future? What you want to do with your life?"

"No, not really. What about you?"

The question he repeated back dazed her. "Um, no, other than to get enough work to make a decent living and keep the house running."

He nodded and the screen door slammed shut behind him. She latched the door, watched him enter his new car and squeal off leaving clouds of red dust in front of the house.

Lei sat on the couch and brought her knees up to her chest. She didn't have a plan like Jess did. Maybe the time had come. She toyed with her ponytail, as if it could relieve her concerns.

She'd put all thoughts of a future with someone to rest after Eric. Jess came to mind, but he shouldn't have. Not an option. She bit the inside of her cheek with much to ponder about her life.

A loud knock made the screen door clatter again. "It's Jess."

"Hi. I'll unlatch the hook." She opened it for him to enter.

"Glad you keep it locked." His brows rushed together. "You haven't had any more unwanted visitors have you?"

Her tone intensified. "No, thank heavens."

"Good. Remember, it's the security investigator in me. I had to ask." Jess entered the kitchen and surveyed the living area. "You've done a lot so far. Looks like a different house."

"Thanks." She motioned for him to sit at the kitchen table. "Let's have a look at the fabric. First things first."

He sat and pulled the chair closer to the table. His eyebrows raised. "All these choices?"

Lei's lips curved up at the edges, her voice robust. "Yeah. I wanted to bring along as much fabric as I could for future needs. I'll be set for a while."

Jess caught her gaze. "Impressive." He moved the fabric swatches around and pointed at one. "I like this geometric tapa cloth pattern. Looks masculine with the brown and black for a tablecloth and two sofa pillows. And I'll take another tablecloth in this pineapple pattern." Jess looked up and pointed toward the living room area. "Did you make those chair covers, too?"

She tilted her head to the side. "I did. Do they look okay?"

"Yeah. Sign me up for two." He studied the fabrics again. "I'll take this tan one and this two-tone grayish one."

Was he ordering out of pity for her not having stable work? No, so far Jess proved decent, genuine. "I should have them for you in less than a week." She gathered the large bolts she needed for his order and placed them near the sewing machine. How nice of him to place an order and even suggest the crafts at the hotel and a pastor, too. Never knowing anyone like him, she couldn't contain a large, grin.

Hands against the edge of the table, he scooted his chair back and straightened his legs. "Great, but you don't have to hurry."

"I won't, but I do have the time now." She returned to the table. "I don't have much work so far. I posted a few pamphlets around Lahaina advertising mending and sewing small items, but it hasn't proved helpful yet. Maybe I should take out an ad in the *Maui News*."

"It might help." He bounced a curled knuckle at his lips. "What will you plan to do if the mending doesn't work out well enough for you?"

Lei wet her lips and fidgeted with her hands. She didn't have special skills or much work experience besides sewing. College hadn't been an option for her right after foster care. "I have no idea what else I could do or who would hire me for anything." She gazed up at him. "This will sound crazy, but I had a dream not long ago and I sold items I made like purses, placemats, even clothes for *keikis,* but only the little kids. My own small business. The problem is, I wouldn't know where to start with renting a shop, let alone afford the rent for it. I can't even grow my mending work. It was a dream, all wishful thinking."

Jess scratched his chin and paused. "Hmm. Not necessarily. There's a first time for everything."

She rolled her eyes. "Yeah, tell me about it as a first time home owner. The costs associated with turning on the utilities and house insurance invited me into the real world. I'm so grateful for this home, but I've learned a lot in the last few weeks."

With elbows on the table, he rested his chin in his hands. "Know what? I've got a feeling you'll do fine."

A beacon of hope, the man gave her support. A new, pleasant experience for her. She so wanted to believe him. "Thanks. Nice of you to say."

"I'm serious. You don't have to rent a building to have a lucrative business. And with a website you can reach a lot of people to buy your products, too." Jess raised his head and leaned closer. "Tell you what. Why don't you come to a church service with me at the Hawaiian Hotel on my day off? There's a special Saturday service this coming weekend. I can show you where the local artisans sell their Hawaiian products. See what you think. And we'll have lunch afterwards."

The man was an absolute blessing. Too good to be true? "Sure can't hurt. Why not?" The comments Jess made the other day about searching for people entered Lei's mind. Her voice softened. "I told you I wasn't interested in genealogy or the DNA website, but I do have a missing piece in my life."

He caught her gaze. "Go ahead."

"My father." She wrung her hands. "For a long time I didn't want to know what happened to him after he left us. What if he'd ended up worse off than when living on Maui, or straightened out and had a nice home life unlike ours here? I couldn't face it. But now it might give me closure to deal with it and move ahead with my life. I have a new home, live in a different town, and I'm trying to make a fresh start."

His eyes widened as if he could relate. "I can help you if you'd like. Believe me, I totally understand."

Her brows furrowed. "Is your father estranged from you, too?"

Jess lowered his head and stared at the table. "No, my father passed away."

She squeezed her eyes shut a moment. "I'm so sorry. I shouldn't have asked."

"It's okay. He's been gone for a long time." Jess rose. "Pick you up Saturday, a little before eight?"

"Umm, okay. Sounds good." How great to have a sliver of hope.

"See you then." He headed out the door.

She latched the screen door again, returned to the table and piled the extra swatches of cloth and returned them with the extra bolts of fabric to the bedroom.

When he asked to pick her up Saturday, she'd considered replying to him it was a date, but stopped herself. They weren't dating. Yet in a way it did qualify as an actual date, but not in the romantic sense. Why would she even think of such a thing? Jess planned to move away in time. Lei remembered this was business and friendship. Making a decent living came first for her now, period.

Lei rubbed the tension from her neck. Kimo's words also gave her something more to consider. What did she truthfully want to do with her life?

Some of the words from Jeremiah 29:11 came to mind. *For I know the plans I have for you...plans to give you hope and a future.*

Did God really have a plan for her future? She hoped so. For now she'd take one step at a time in her current situation, and try to deal with what life continued to bring her way.

CHAPTER FOUR

On Saturday morning, seven-thirty a.m. Lei sat in the kitchen and tapped her fingers on the table. She and Jess would only attend the church service and tour the resort. A simple event, yet she couldn't settle herself. He'd talked about lunch, too, which wasn't necessary.

The screen door clattered. She bolted from the table to answer it. "Oh. Come in, Mrs. Chen."

The small woman entered and put a sack on the table. "Aloha. Good morning, I have cinnamon rolls today."

"Mahalo. You're spoiling me with your baked goods." She pulled out a kitchen chair for Mrs. Chen.

"I won't stay long. Jess says he's taking you to where he works today. I think he's excited about it."

What did it mean? "Yes, I'm hoping I can sell my sewing goods there. I definitely need the employment."

Mrs. Chen gazed at the living room. "You make those slipcovers?"

"Yes, and this tablecloth." She pinched the fabric between her fingers. "I can do placemats and pillows, and if I get additional work I'll consider making purses and more."

The woman eyed the pattern and applique before her on the table. "Nice. You got business cards? I can pass them around. Here, we take care of each other. And Jess, I think he likes to watch after you, too."

Her eyes widened. What did Mrs. Chen mean? She folded her hands to keep them at rest. "No, I don't have business cards. It's an excellent idea. I'll order some soon. As for Jess, remember he's a security guard. Looking out for others comes naturally for him." What had she gotten herself into?

Another rap on the screen door. Jess poked his head inside the house. "Hi ladies. Lei, are you ready?"

"Yes." She stood and ignored the muscle twitch near her eye.

Mrs. Chen bid them good-bye.

At the Hawaiian Hotel, they walked through the beautiful, Hawaiian-themed hotel registration area adorned with red anthurium arrangements, a set of ancient drums, and Hawaiian artifacts. Lei stopped to absorb it all. "What a beautiful job they've done displaying the Hawaiian culture. So impressive."

"Wait until you see the courtyard." Jess extended his arm and led her onto the grounds. Trade winds swept over them and mynah birds squawked in the trees above.

She shaded her eyes from the sun. "I've never been to any resort before, and I've lived on Maui all my life." She glanced at the *kukui* nuts on the ground from the candlewood tree, numerous varieties of plumeria and a young koa tree. So comfortable walking with Jess now. Why had she been so nervous about coming? "I'm impressed they've used some of the area for trees and plants grown in Hawaii." A banana tree heavily laden with fruit and a taro patch nearby also spoke of Maui. "How wonderful, especially for visitors not from this precious island to learn and experience."

Jess touched her shoulder. "I thought you'd appreciate these gardens, but I want to head to the lobby so you can see the area where the artisans set up their wares."

She couldn't wait. Trade winds rippled her blue dress as she entered the foyer. "Wow. Look at these fine crafts." A chipping noise echoed from the wood splitting as a carver chiseled away. A sewing machine hummed while a lady stitched a Hawaiian-patterned muʻumuʻu next to a display of aloha shirts on the table in front of her for sale.

Jess tilted his head toward her. "Could you see yourself here?"

Her heart pounded as she imagined what it would be like. "Maybe. I don't know. I'd like to think so."

He fiddled in his pocket until he pulled out a business card. "If you do, here's the man you need to call for all the details. The products are all Hawaiian crafted by local artisans. You fit the criteria and it's an easy and inexpensive way to start a business."

Accepting the card from him, she grazed his fingers. A slight chill rushed through her and a tear welled in her eye. "Thanks so much, Jess."

"Sure. Let's go out to the gazebo for the church service."

As she walked outside, her mind raced. Jess had arranged in advance to obtain the business card as well as set this invitation up for her. But life had taught her people often did something for you, if they wanted something back. So was he extra caring and thoughtful, or did he have an agenda and want to control her like Eric?

Pastor's helpers handed out pink plumeria blossoms with a toothpick inserted for the ladies to put behind the appropriate ear, signifying if married or single. Heat crept into her face as she positioned the flower behind her right ear, indicating her single status. Jess smiled at her as they sat in folding chairs in the gazebo's shade.

The pastor came to the lectern. A tall, stocky Hawaiian man, probably in his sixties, wearing a tapa cloth designed shirt with gray hair pulled back in a ponytail and a beard, smiled at all of them.

"I'm Pastor Pu'a Kane. Aloha. Welcome." He picked up his 'ukulele and strummed a hymn. Next, Pastor Kane's message spoke volumes regarding living God's will in lieu of one's own. Easier said than done. After powerful prayer, the service ended and the pastor opened his arms wide. "And remember folks, you're too blessed to be stressed."

Smiling, she gazed at Jess.

"Ready to go?" He grinned back at her.

The nearby table outside the gazebo area offered information about the pastor and church. She collected some brochures. He'd impressed her and she needed a new church home.

"Let's walk along the ocean, down to the Monkeypod Kitchen Restaurant." He held out his arm for her.

"Oh, you don't have to take me anywhere else. This has been wonderful."

His brow raised. "I want to and besides, I promised you. It's only lunch."

It sounded reasonable when he said it now. She'd made too much of it. "Okay, lunch it is."

As they strode along the walkway arm in arm, the ocean roared and showed high tide with wet sand over most of the beach. How comforting to walk along with him. Could this be real?

People chattered in the lively, upscale restaurant as they walked to a table in the rear.

She sat across from Jess and wrung her hands, never having been in such a nice restaurant. "This is quite fancy, but I do like the open air and it's right here on the beach. Nice."

The waitress dropped off menus and brought them water.

"I hoped you'd like it." He picked up the menu.

"You had this particular restaurant planned, too." Her back stiffened. He'd set up everything.

"We'd talked about stopping after the service, and I'd found this place beforehand, since it's close to work. I stop in here now and then."

After Lei picked up the menu, she gasped. "Nothing's inexpensive here at all, compared to what I'm used to ordering."

"My treat. I suggested it. It's reasonable for the great restaurant it is and not something a person does every day. Have whatever you like."

Staring at the menu, she'd order a small plate. She wouldn't take advantage of the situation and also didn't want to feel she owed Jess anything. Why should he buy her an expensive meal after all he'd done for her at the hotel earlier?

The waitress returned and took their orders.

"Tell me about you and your family." Jess focused his gaze on Lei. "Since we're neighbors, I'd like to get to know you better."

She drew in a breath. "I was born and raised on Maui and don't ever intend to leave it. My mom was Hawaiian and taught me to sew when I was seven. She worked as a seamstress in a shop in Lahaina. My dad came from the mainland. He got into drugs when I was young. When the going got tough, he left us and headed back to the mainland. We didn't know what happened to him, where he resided and never heard from him again. Mom took ill and passed away not too long after he left. We grew up in foster care, as our grandmother didn't have the means to take us in at the time. I've continued sewing for work since high school."

His brows bunched. "So sorry to hear this. It must've been difficult."

"Thank you, but it was a long time ago. I have a wonderful grandmother and two siblings. I guess it's why I often look forward, not back, when I can." How easy to speak with Jess. Too easy. She tilted her head. "And you?"

"Born on Oahu and lived there through junior high. When my dad ended his military career, we returned to the mainland. I took a job tending horses at a big estate during high school and for a short while afterwards. I floundered around. Then I finally went to criminal justice school and police science training. I worked for a while, took on some additional training and now I'm ticking away time to return to my roots on Oahu and a special criminal investigation job."

What did floundering mean? She had no reason to ask what he meant. "It sounds like you have your life in order. What did you think of the pastor's comments of living our life for God's plan?"

"I admit I've had my own personal agenda in my life and now in setting up my career." He leaned back in the chair. "I'm not sure if it's God's plan, but I'd like to think so."

"I don't think my life is God's plan so far, either. We'll see what happens with my basic employment for starters, let alone God's work in my life."

Jess's warm hand squeezed her forearm. Even with the late summer heat, his warmth and strength radiated through her, yet she shivered at his touch.

"Does it mean you're considering applying at the Hawaiian Hotel?" He moved in closer.

She stared into his sea-green eyes, the same color as the ocean beyond the shoreline nearby. "Yes, I think I will."

"Great." He took both of her hands in his. "I know it'll work out for you. Your creations are as good as any in the hotel lobby if not better."

A warm flush crept across her cheeks. Did he believe in her or only being nice to her? "I'm afraid to get my hopes up so we'll wait and see. Thanks so much for suggesting it."

Would she run into Jess at the hotel if she worked there? He'd made it clear what he wanted in life, yet he drew her attention.

After they finished their meal and returned home, Mrs. Chen entered Lei's yard.

"Afternoon, Mrs. Chen."

The woman's tan face displayed a frown. "I came to tell you I saw a young, slender teenage girl skulking around. Long blonde hair to the middle of her back. Looked through several windows and stood at the front door of your house. She finally left. Maybe it's somebody you know. If not, I thought I should tell you. I've seen more people around here in the last few weeks, than in the past six months."

Could it be? She scratched her chin. "Mahalo, Mrs. Chen. I'll check into it."

The woman nodded and stepped across the tufted grass toward her house.

Once inside, Lei called her brother. "Did Elle come by to see me today, Kimo?"

He groaned. "She's been here all day."

"Oh. Okay."

His voice rose. "Why would you think she'd show up today?"

Now, she'd roused Kimo's curiosity. She squeezed the phone. "My neighbor said someone came to the door and the description fit Elle. I wanted to follow up with her if she did come by."

"She didn't. What kind of neighbors do you have, anyway?" He chuckled. "A bunch of busy bodies?"

"No, the neighbors like to help each other out if they can. We'll talk again."

"All right, sis."

Now the question remained, who would come looking around her house? Elle's the only one Lei knew who would fit the description, but why would Kimo say she didn't come if she had? Or maybe a stranger wondered about having some mending done. But she'd never given her address out on the flyers.

Lei would focus on planning her sewing creations and concentrating on an interview with the manager at the Hawaiian Hotel. But she'd keep her eyes and ears open when at home.

CHAPTER FIVE

Later in the afternoon, Jess sat in the kitchen, stared out the window and drummed his fingers on the table.

What an awesome morning with Lei. She was everything a man could want. Bright, beautiful, compassionate and loving despite the heartache and difficulties she'd endured in her younger years. Amazing.

He stared at the laptop on the table and opened it. Time to come back to the real world. He'd check Facebook again in case he could find Paula's name.

The phone buzzed. "Hi, Mom. Good to hear your voice."

"Yours, too. How are you doing?"

"Great." He closed the laptop. "I like the work I'm doing well enough, have a decent house and nice neighbors."

"Oh, good, Jess. You don't know how much it means to me."

He blew out a breath. "There's no need to worry about me. I'm fine."

"Son, I miss you, but I think you made the right decision to start a new life away from all the heartache you had here. And I'm glad you're focusing on what you want for a change and not making your life all about others. Are you planning to go to Oahu yet, or do you like Maui?"

He pushed the kitchen chair back, stepped over to the sofa and sat. "I definitely like Maui, but the job I want is on Oahu. It'll pay better and allow me to use more of my training, too. I can't do the same here."

"Sounds reasonable." She paused. "Jess, you're not continuing to look for Paula are you?"

And there was the usual and dreaded question. He squeezed his eyes shut. "Mom, I'm not looking for Paula to pursue a relationship with her again, so don't worry."

Mom's pitch became jarring. "But you're looking for her. How do you expect to move on with your life? When will this end?"

He clenched his teeth and his chest tightened. "When I find out the truth for certain and take the responsibility I've had kept from me." He pinched the bridge of his nose and hoped to stave off the tension building in his forehead. How to make her understand?

Mom's voice came across loud and shrill. "For heaven's sake, you were in high school and have done everything you could for years now. As long as Mr. Jules is alive you'll never accomplish anything. You were only a servant in his viewpoint and will remain so in his opinion. He'll never let you be involved in any aspect of his family. And even if you could reach Paula, he'd make it hard on the both of you. You know this. Let it go."

His mother was upset and so was he, but he wouldn't lie to her. His voice boomed. "I can't forget a child. I won't."

31

"You're wasting your time. You don't even know if it's yours."

Mom's words pierced his heart. "I saw the baby in the hospital right after she was born. The dates coincide with my relationship with Paula, if you're looking for facts."

"It isn't a fact. Besides, corresponding dates guarantee nothing. It doesn't mean the child is yours. For all you know, maybe the infant was placed for adoption, regardless of whoever fathered it."

His stomach lurched and his heart raced at the notion. "Let's agree to disagree. I don't want to argue with you, Mom, and I don't want any connection with the Jules family. But I do have a right to know the truth someday, so I keep my options open. It's a small part of my life right now. I told you I'm doing great and I am." Unable to calm himself, he gritted his teeth.

"Have you met anyone yet? I mean a special lady?"

Maybe Mom would settle down a little if he told her about Lei. "I've met a nice woman, but it's a friendship at this point."

"Wonderful. This is the first girl you've mentioned to me since Paula. I hope it's something more than what you're telling me."

"I haven't known her long." He scratched his chin. "We'll see in time. She's from Maui, born and raised, and loves it here. But I'll leave sometime in the future so it's hard to say."

Mom's voice quivered. "I only want what's best for you, Jess."

He huffed out a breath. "I know you do, Mom. Remember, I made the choice and distanced myself from the overall situation. I got over Paula a long time ago. Love you."

"I love you, too. We'll talk again soon."

Jess sprawled out on the couch. A wealthy and powerful man, Mr. Jules controlled everyone in his path, even his own family. If nothing else, Jess agreed with Mom about this one point.

He and Paula were way too young, and they'd gotten more involved than they should have. They were human and made a mistake. But once Paula told him about the pregnancy he stood by his responsibility, regardless of how many ways Mr. Jules shoved him out of Paula's life.

Yet God took a difficult situation and made something good from it, a precious baby girl. He closed his eyes, recalling the precious few moments near her at the hospital.

He'd surprised himself by talking about Lei to his mother. Jess laced his hands behind his neck and tipped his head back. Could she be the one for him? Way too soon to consider it. Had he acted too fast?

Right now she needed to settle into her work and life, too, as he did. Best not to get too close if they wanted dissimilar paths in life, let alone live on different islands. And what about his seven-year-old child?

Complications never helped and required addressing first. He'd make an effort to take his time with Lei, but he couldn't get her out of his mind.

*

Lei found it hard to believe a week had passed since she gained approval to work at the Hawaiian Hotel. Late in the afternoon, she inventoried the display of items for sale on the table in front of her. Sales remained high throughout the first week. She loved the new job so far, but now she needed to sew like crazy and create more inventory. With the sale table closed, she packed her remaining sewing creations into a suitcase.

She headed out the lobby door and stepped into the heat. Pastor Puʻa Kane met her on the sidewalk.

He stopped. "Miss Hudson, isn't it?"

"Yes. Leilani Hudson. Nice to see you again Pastor Kane. I'm so glad to have found a new church home."

The pastor wiped sweat from his brow. "You're more than welcome. How's the new job going?"

"Great. If I hadn't had help from some of the people I've met around here it wouldn't have turned out so well for me, or maybe not at all. I'm not comfortable depending on others, but I'm so grateful."

Pastor Kane extended his arm toward the shady bench under the pink plumeria tree.

Lei took a seat, glad to escape the heat for a moment.

The pastor sat next to her. "Yes, we all need others. If we see folks as separate or different in life, they can become a threat. But if we see them as part of us, connected, we can face any challenge together."

She hadn't thought of people before in such a way. "I guess it makes sense."

"If it weren't for others, we couldn't do much of anything on our own if you think about it. God wired us for communion with others and Himself, you know."

As she stared at the resort's waterfall tumbling down on the lava rocks, memories of why she couldn't depend on others flooded her mind. People would come and go in life. But God and her homeland of Maui gave her a sense of stability and a place to belong. Neither of them ever failed her like people had. "Yes, but it's not easy for me. My heart lies with the land and of course, God, especially when life gets rough."

He turned toward her. "It's good you have a relationship with God but remember the land, beautiful as it is here and sacred to us Hawaiians isn't our permanent home. God has a world much more magnificent for us. In the meantime, He wishes for us to follow His will."

"I understand, but it's hard for me to let go and follow Him."

"It's hard for everybody, Lei. We all think we're in control of our lives, but we're truly not. Things happen sometimes to make us face it." He pointed an index finger toward his chest. "Look at me. I'm tired today, it's hot and I'm ready to go home. But I feel God wants me to go visit at the prison now. I don't feel like going so much, but I want to and I will."

She gazed into Pastor Kane's smiling eyes. "Thanks. I needed to hear this today."

"Good. I'm glad. Anytime Miss Hudson, anytime at all." He stood and shook her hand.

As the pastor walked away, a car came up the driveway, and the bellboy walked over to greet the driver. Even the hotel had a community of staff working together in order to serve others, when she stopped to think about it. She tapped an index finger against her lip. Hmm, depending on people, a totally new experience. Could it work for her now when it hadn't before?

Lei headed toward the parking ramp in the hot Hawaiian sun for the drive home. She'd have plenty to think about while sewing all evening.

When she arrived at the house, she removed the suitcase from the trunk and looked through the hibiscus bushes hoping to

35

spot Jess's car. He wasn't home yet, so she entered the cool plantation house and placed the suitcase near the sewing machine in the living room.

The man was too good to be true and deserved her thanks for the information and opportunity he'd presented her for work at the hotel. Helpful and kind, she'd depended on him, but why did he help her? People didn't do something for nothing, did they? She couldn't let the idea go.

Maybe in time she'd try to be open and adjust to this new life and attitude she found with Jess, if it continued in a positive light.

After changing into shorts and a T-shirt, she sat at the machine and sewed placemats. They'd sold the best so far, small and easy to pack for tourists.

A few hours later she stretched her arms above her head. Time had slipped by and she needed a break. Walking to the fridge, she clicked open a cola, took out the leftover pepperoni pizza and heated it. The delicious, spicy flavor tasted great, followed by the cold cola. Refreshed, she headed back to the machine, wanting to create as much inventory as possible tonight.

Only the hum of the sewing disturbed the quiet of the house. When she finished the quota of placemats, darkness had arrived. A glance at her wristwatch revealed the time as nine-thirty. She gazed back towards the kitchen. The rest of the house had no lamps illuminated.

Maybe she'd give Jess a call now and thank him regarding her job before it got much later. She headed toward the kitchen to switch on the light.

A loud bang echoed on the bedroom side of the house. She jolted back and her heart thumped as she grabbed the phone and punched in Jess's number.

"What's up, Lei?"

Her voice trembled. "I heard a booming noise outside my bedroom."

"Stay put. I'll be right over."

With only the light of the sewing machine on, she sat on the couch, legs weak and shaky. The phone buzzed and she bolted upward.

"Hi, Malia. I can't talk right now. Jess is coming over. I heard a noise outside. He'll be here any second."

"Has Eric bothered you again?"

She tucked her knees up to her chest. "No. It's probably nothing. I'll talk to you tomorrow."

"Call me if you need me."

A knock on the kitchen door. "It's Jess."

Lei hurried to the door. "Thanks for coming. I haven't heard anything more. Now I feel silly."

"You shouldn't." Jess shut the door behind him and relocked it. "The cops are coming. It doesn't hurt to check it out and it's good to have it on record."

"I admit I do get a little excited if there's a commotion. I had someone vandalize my apartment twice and break my window not too long ago in Kahului. A huge lava rock missed my head by a few feet. The landlord figured it was some issue or revenge against me and raised my rent. It's why I had to move out." The words fell out of her mouth.

His voice rose. "What?"

"No big deal. It wasn't Eric. A teenager claimed he got paid by someone to do it, but I'm jumpy at noises yet."

Jess took a hold of her shoulders and gave a slight squeeze. "I'm glad you called me. It's a good to tell the police about this incident and the apartment vandalism, since they're similar. I didn't see or hear anything when I walked across from my house. Think I'll take a look out the bedroom window. Don't want to walk on footprints or any evidence. We'll wait for the police."

She stood at the bedroom door, hands trembling. Would Eric do something like this? Not his style. Her ex-boyfriend might not be unhinged, yet his past behavior had pushed the line. And why would a teenager come to Lahaina after being caught in Kahului? A muscle twitched in her jaw.

Jess knelt down along the windowsill and took a peek under the window shade. "I don't see anyone now." He shone a pencil flashlight straight down near the bottom of the window.

"Looks like clumps of dirt near the edge of the house. I don't see anything else. Someone must've run off after they made the noise."

"How strange." She pressed a palm over the throbbing pulse in her throat. "Why would someone do such a thing?"

He stood, came toward her and hugged her. "Good question. It looks deliberate. With the house dark, maybe someone thought you weren't here. After the police investigate, I'll put up a few motion detector lights for you tomorrow. And then we'll see about some deadbolts, too."

"No, I couldn't let you." She pulled back.

His voice rose. "Why not? Don't you want to know if someone's on the property at night?"

She turned and headed toward the couch. He had a point.

Jess followed right behind her at her heels.

"You've done so much for me already." Lei sat on the end of the sofa and tapped her foot on the floor. An empty feeling came from the pit of her stomach. "I can't expect any more from you."

"But I offered, and it isn't a big deal. It's not costly, if that's what you're worried about." Jess took a seat on the other end of the couch.

"No, I wasn't concerned about the cost."

"Then what's the problem? Tell me." He leaned closer to her.

She wrung her hands and stared downward. "I'm not used to expecting so much help from people and feeling beholden to them."

Jess cocked his head to the side. "You think you would owe me something? I don't expect anything back from you. Please don't ever feel that way, okay?"

"This is all new to me. So many changes at once. It's too much. I can't think right now." A shiver ran across the back of her neck. How surprising to think the first person she called was Jess for his help and not the police.

The law enforcement vehicle's siren rang.

Jess studied her face in silence.

Lei hadn't intended to offend him, but he'd asked the question and she'd answered it. She fidgeted on the sofa. "I'll go let the officers into the house."

CHAPTER SIX

The next afternoon, Lei sat in the living room chair, legs curled under her. She'd forgotten to call Malia about the noise outside last night. A glance at her watch showed plenty of time left before Jess came home from work and installed the motion detector lights. She grabbed the phone and punched in her sister's number.

"I've been waiting for your call. What happened last night?"

She leaned her head back on the chair. "Sorry, Malia. I worked all day. I don't have much of an answer for you anyway."

Malia's voice lilted upward. "What do you mean?"

"Someone dug an area around the bedroom window and took off. I don't know why or what they might've been after, since all the police found was a hole."

"How crazy. It doesn't make any sense."

"Yeah, Jess and I thought so, too. Pretty insane." She scratched her head and shifted in the chair.

"I can tell you who wasn't there."

40

Lei brows raised. Please let her assumption be incorrect. "What are you talking about?"

"After I spoke to you I took a drive by Eric's house and—"

Lei's voice thundered and her heart skipped a beat. "You what?"

"He's bothered you so much. Plus, you've had a rock thrown through the apartment window and now a hole dug in your yard. I worried, and I had to know if he could've been involved."

What had Malia done? Lei sat upright, her spine straight as a new pencil. "The last thing you need is for him to harass you. What if he'd been there and saw you? Malia, you shouldn't have done it. Now I'm worried for you. It's the kind of thing which sets him off."

"He was home, but I doubt he realized who I was. Even if he did, it's not a crime to drive by a house and turn around."

"It may not be a crime, but we're talking about Eric." She lowered her head and closed her eyes for a moment, but couldn't calm herself. "I know you meant well, but for your own good, stay away from him and his house, please."

"I will, but now we know it wasn't him."

Time to change the subject. "Have you seen Kimo and Elle?" She massaged the back of her stiff neck.

"Not since Dirk gave each of them a room to stay in at his house."

A surprise, but a nice one. "I didn't know they moved. Nice of Dirk to take them in, especially with Tutu selling her and Henry's home and her upcoming move to assisted living. We'll know where Kimo and Elle can be reached, anyhow."

"Yeah, my thoughts, too. Dirk said he'll continue to help Tutu with her finances, since Henry's gone. Another relief."

41

"Exactly." She glanced out the kitchen window. "Jess's car is in the driveway. He's installing some motion detector lights for me. Talk to you soon."

The screen door creaked as Lei opened it. A drill buzzed. A walk through the backyard into the afternoon heat revealed an installed lamp and Jess standing under it looking rugged in a white T-shirt and brown shorts.

He wiped his brow. "What do you think?"

"Perfect. Thank you."

Jess pointed. "Come over and look at this hole. I dug around the area to see if I could find anything."

She darted across the yard and stared into the opening. "What is it?"

He removed the ladder from the side of the house. "I wondered it if might be something ancient." He bent over. "See these smooth lava rocks aligned?"

Lei placed her hand over her brows to shade her view. "Yeah."

"It might be an ancient Hawaiian *heiau* site. Can't tell, though. Do you want me to leave the area open in case it is?"

Reminders of the incident weren't welcome. "No, I'd rather have it covered for now. But I can check to find out if it was once a sacred site or temple."

Jess used the shovel to move some of the dirt back over the rocks. "Good idea." He smoothed the remainder of the dirt level with the grass. "I've got one more light to install."

"I'll go inside and bring you something to drink."

"Great." He carried the ladder around the corner of the house.

As she paced across the grass, the wind caught her hair and the smell of the plumeria filled her nostrils. Jess to the rescue again.

Inside, she took two plastic tumblers from the cabinet and filled them with ice. She poured the tea into them and the ice crackled. Nothing better than iced tea on a hot, Hawaiian summer day. Jess deserved more, but she was thankful for his help and had admitted he'd been correct about the lights.

She picked up both cups, opened the screen door and headed out toward the front of the house. Both tumblers dropped from her hands and banged on the sidewalk at the sight of him. "Eric. What do you want?"

Eric glanced at the wet sidewalk in front of her and smirked. "I see you remain a klutz. Or do I have a powerful effect on you?"

She trembled and realized why he'd come. "Please leave."

Eric stepped closer to her, his voice deep. "Not until I make something clear. Do not, I repeat, do not send your sister around to do your spying."

Lei wanted to die inside. "I didn't. I don't want anything from you. Leave Malia out of this. She means no harm."

His voice exploded. "Do you understand what I said?" He pushed his palm hard against her shoulder.

Sweat trickled down her forehead as Lei swayed to regain her balance. She clenched her fists and drew in a breath to keep her voice strong. She hated to kowtow to Eric, but Malia's wellbeing came first. "Definitely. She won't be around again. I'll make certain of it."

Jess's voice thundered from behind. "Keep your hands off her."

Eric's sickening smirk returned, and he faced Jess. "Or what big guy? Gonna threaten me? Good luck, dude. You'll need it. I don't take orders from you and I come out on top in any situation. Got it?"

"Maybe you'll take orders from the police." Jess pulled the phone out of his pocket.

Acid churning in her stomach, Lei couldn't even move.

Eric turned toward Lei. "Keep her and her sister in hand. They don't have anything I want. I've got much better waiting for me." Eric glared at her as if she'd turned into road kill. He turned and swaggered across the yard to his car.

Jess hugged her.

With her arms around his waist, she trembled. "I'm sorry, Jess. I'll explain later about him mentioning Malia."

He pulled back, but his hands continued to rest on her shoulders. "You don't have to if you don't want. But this guy is bad news all the way around. I'm putting those deadbolts in tomorrow. Security cameras wouldn't hurt either."

Lei picked up the tumblers from the sidewalk and Jess followed her into the kitchen. He sat at the kitchen table while she filled two more glasses with tea. She slid one across the table for Jess and took a seat.

Words tumbled from her mouth in a rush. "Malia called me right after I heard the noise and I told her about it right before you came over last evening. She told me today she drove by Eric's place last night to see if he was home. He obviously noticed her or her car since he has lights and cameras all around and of course, showed up here because of it."

Jess threw his head back. "Oh, brother. You need to call Malia and tell her what happened here, so she knows to stay clear of him."

Her fingers rubbed against the condensation on the outside of the cold glass. "When I talked to her earlier this afternoon, I told Malia she shouldn't have done it. What if Eric confronts her, too? I'll let her know soon."

"Good idea." He sipped the tea. "Between his actions and the odd stuff occurring lately, it's best to stay aware."

She bit her bottom lip. "I know. Malia will agree, too."

"I don't mean to worry you more, but we'll make sure you have security here." Jess squeezed her forearm.

Now it came down to more security. Her mind swarmed like a disturbed beehive. How did it come to this? Lei repositioned herself in the chair. "I don't understand why people such as Eric can't leave others alone. Yet when I wanted to belong somewhere, as when in foster care, I couldn't fit in the way I'd hoped. If it wasn't for my living here now, thanks to you and Mrs. Chen, I'd feel out of place or lost most of the time. I truly like people, but I rarely have a common bond with them, yet I thought I had one with Eric of all people. What does it say about me?" She lowered her head. "I suppose I should take responsibility for it, too."

"You're a wonderful person. Don't let Eric win by getting you down on yourself. It's what he wants. If you do, you let him have power over you." Jess reached across the table and gripped her hand. "You've had some hard times, and you were right before when you said you didn't want to look back at the tough periods too often. Life should move uphill from here. It has to get better. I'm sure it will."

"Thanks, Jess. I'm not ordinarily this down and out. You're right. I know it in my head, but last night's and today's incidents got to me. Sorry."

Jess's words sounded promising, and she needed to work hard at believing them, especially in situations like this. Yet she harbored concerns of what might happen next in life. So many odd occurrences made her skeptical. Why did they happen around her? First the apartment incidents and now the digging in the yard.

Regardless, she needed to move forward and deal with them as best as she could. Jess said life would move upward. She was more than ready.

*

After work the following afternoon, Jess leaned over and finished installing the last deadbolt on Lei's kitchen door. He stood, dusted off his hands and pointed to the lock. "There. Now you're set." He closed the door, turned the deadbolt over with a click and took a seat across from her at the kitchen table.

"Thanks. I want to pay you now." She dug into her purse.

"If you insist, but only for the cost of the locks on the receipt right here on the table. It was my idea to install them." Jess wanted to provide this simple task, but he understood Lei needed to feel independent, too.

After glancing at the receipt, she handed him the cash. "Here you are."

He shoved the bills in his wallet. "I think you should consider checking into Eric's harassment, like what you can do about it in addition to a restraining order, especially if he bothers you again."

Her tone increased. "And how much will it cost? What can anyone do?"

"Maybe they have ways to keep him at bay, or even arrest him if he keeps doing this. I'm not sure. It's why I think you need to find out." He folded his hands on the table and leaned forward. "You might not have to pay a lot for the information if you do some research online, make calls and check out fees. Then if he does bother you again, you'll have the information at hand."

She scooted the chair back. "I'll think about it, but I wouldn't know where to start."

"I can give you some info." He'd told her once more what to do. What if she thought he wanted to control or make her dependent on him again? "But only if you want. Your decision."

"Fine."

"I only state what I think are helpful suggestions. I'd never try to control your life. I hope you understand my intentions."

Her gaze met his. "Why do you make the suggestions, Jess?"

Jess's heart boomed against his rib cage. He'd become more serious, and she deserved an honest answer. He rubbed his sweaty palms together and hoped his statement wouldn't scare her away. "I care about people and I like to help them. It's why I chose the job I have, too." He paused and drew in a breath. "I care about you. A lot." There he'd said it. Put his heart out to her.

She sat motionless, but her eyes widened. "You don't have to say such a thing."

The past had shredded her trust. She didn't believe him. His eye twitched, and he wrung his hands. "I know, but I wanted to say it since it's true. I've never known anyone like you."

47

"And I haven't met someone as kind and special as you are. But every day I think you're too good to be true."

He chuckled, reached across the table and squeezed her hands. "I make my mistakes, but I've been honest about my feelings for you. I hope you can trust me on this in time. You'll see. I won't turn on you the way Eric did or walk away on a whim if a few problems arise."

She tipped her head to the side. "You know about my past, my life. It's not easy for me to change overnight. In fact you know more about me than I do about you."

He stood, came around the table and lifted her to her feet. "We can easily fix it right now. Ask away." He placed his hands around her shoulders, drew her close and touched her hair. The silkiness of it in his hand, her soft breath against his cheek drove him crazy. He touched the softness of her lip and covered her mouth with his, mindless.

She pulled back. "Let's go outside and sit, since it's fairly cool out for a change."

Breathless, he shook his head and followed her out the door. He needed to cool it. "It's nice out here. The plumeria and palm trees hide most of Front Street, but you can hear the ocean. It's so quiet without any noisy traffic."

They sat in the old, paint-chipped aluminum chairs in front of the house.

She turned toward him. "Yeah. I definitely appreciate having this home."

The trade winds gusted and helped him feel more refreshed. Should he offer to answer questions about his life? Might as well. He hadn't planned what he'd said earlier tonight either, regarding his feelings for her. "Did you want to know anything specific about me? I think I've told you about my family, where I lived and my education."

"Yes, it sounds like a good life." She turned and faced him. "But you mentioned you floundered after high school. What did you mean?"

His pulse pounded in his ears. He had to tell the truth or she'd never trust him. But would it turn her away from him? "It's kind of a long story."

She gazed into his eyes. "I've got time."

"Remember, I told you I worked at a large estate. I made a huge mistake. One I'm sorry for, learned from, but can't change how it affected others."

"Go on."

After seeing her brows draw together and her lips in a straight line, he bit the inside of his cheek. A hollowness filled his chest. "I'll start with the basic story. The estate owner was a powerful man. I made the mistake of getting involved with his daughter while I worked there. He tried to control her, and I think in a way she wanted to get away from it. I cared about her and one thing led to another." He lowered his head and paused. "I was the hired help. Her father found out about us, fired me and had me banned from the grounds and his daughter. I had a hard time letting it go and put my life on hold for a while. My parents were upset, too. I finally realized I needed to get some education and take responsibility for my life rather than being overcome with a situation I couldn't change."

With a blank stare and a deep frown, she crossed her arms over her chest. "Have you seen her since then? Do you love her?"

"No to both questions." He turned, placed his hand on the arm of her chair and drew in a much needed breath.

Lei's cell phone buzzed. She held the phone in the palm of her hand and glanced at the screen.

"I should take this. It's my sister."

Jess stood and waved good-bye. Now it was his turn to worry. He shuffled along the tufted grass until he pushed through the hibiscus bushes into his own yard.

Inside, he flipped on the light and fell into a heap in his recliner. He'd bared his soul with Lei tonight. Had it been a mistake? Too much too soon? Maybe she didn't want to hear anymore, which might've partly explained why she took the call.

If he'd stayed with her longer tonight, would he have told her about the pregnancy, now a seven-year-old child? He wanted to think so. Jess grabbed the remote and turned the television set on for some background noise and distraction.

If only he could find Paula, have a DNA match and get this part of his life resolved for absolute certainty. Then he could have something concrete to deal with and discuss, especially with his mother and Lei. Facts in place of assumptions.

He stared at the laptop on the coffee table in front of him.

No, he wouldn't search or check DNA matches in the immediate future. No more impulsiveness as in the past, which led to consequences.

Jess picked up the laptop and set it on top of the dresser in the bedroom.

Lei deserved better, but Jess had dumped a lot on her. He understood she had her own family issues, a new job, the vandalism and Eric's annoyances as challenges, too. She'd fought hard to escape the difficulties in life.

Yet she'd asked him about his background. Should he offer to say more on his own, or wait for her questions? Would she even want a relationship with him now? The look on her face when she asked if he loved Paula pierced his heart.

He walked into the living room, flopped down on the sofa and blew out a breath. Time would tell. For now, he'd give her the space she needed. Her overall welfare came first.

CHAPTER SEVEN

The next afternoon, with another busy day of work behind her, Lei pulled into the dusty driveway. Jess knelt beside her plantation house kitchen window with a board in his hand. Her shoulders tightened, and she tapped a fist against her lips. This couldn't be good. She yanked the car door open and hurried to Jess's side.

Breathless, she stammered. "Don't tell me something—" She covered her mouth with her palm and sucked in a breath. "What is it? What happened?"

With a grim twist to his mouth, he set the boards against the house and stood next to her. "Sorry to say, but someone broke into the house. The police apprehended her."

Lei clutched the purse against her stomach. "Her? Who?"

"Mrs. Chen spotted the girl after hearing glass break." Jess caressed her shoulder. "She took the girl's photo, called the police and said it's the same youthful woman she noticed here in the yard recently."

A warm flush tingled through her, and added to the heat from the sun, making her light-headed. Unable to make sense of it, she met his gaze. "Totally insane."

"Let's go inside the house. I'll finish covering the window in a few minutes to help keep the heat out before the new window arrives. Also, I took it upon myself to order it and have it installed before nightfall, if it's okay. I didn't want to see you staying here tonight without a window. And you have enough to handle."

Knees weak, she ambled into the kitchen and plopped in a chair, her mind reeling from the news. With elbows planted on the table, she held her head in her hands. "I don't know what to say. I'm at a loss."

Jess came to her side and clasped her hand in his. "One good thing, we know it isn't Eric. Do you know anyone who looks like the person Mrs. Chen described to you?"

Lei bit her bottom lip. "No I don't, except for Elle, my brother's girlfriend. But Kimo said she wasn't here on the day when Mrs. Chen said a young blonde woman came by here, so it couldn't be her." She rose and took a quick look around the inside of the house. Nothing appeared damaged or missing at first sight.

"Anything stolen?"

She returned to the kitchen. "No, I don't think so. Without a robbery, this is vandalism, but for what reason?"

With his gaze focused on her, he lifted an eyebrow. "Great question. I hope you find the answer soon. You'll have to go to the police station and see if you can identify the girl. She's being held in Kahului."

"Right. The police station." She blew out a breath and tried to concentrate.

He squeezed her hand tighter. "Do you want me to go along?"

She lifted her chin. "No. I can do it."

"All right. I'll attach the boards now and hopefully have the window replaced when you return. Call me if you need me."

"You've done more than enough. I'm beholden to you once again." She rose and waved good-bye to him.

"No big deal. I happened to come home before you. We all need each other sometimes. Anyone would do the same."

Many would not do the same. Lei entered the car and backed out of the driveway, leaving a trail of red Hawaiian dust. Jess's words stuck in her head. Pastor Kane had said the same thing about needing each other. She'd spent most of her life wanting closeness. No long-term stability came no matter what she did, even as a child. She was grateful for Jess's help again today. But after a lifetime of not expecting much from others, this conflict reared its head for her now when facing problems like this break-in and needing Jess.

She'd deal with her feelings later, yet they'd distracted her from the incident for a moment, which kept her in a tizzy. A break-in right after the yard digging. Unreal.

At the station, an officer led her into a room with a small table and two chairs. "Please sit down, Miss Hudson."

"Thank you." She sat and rubbed her hands over her pant legs and tried to remain calm.

The man opened a folder, took out a picture and held it in front of her. "This is the photo of the woman identified as the person who broke into your house. Do you recognize her?"

Lei's mouth flew open and she gripped the arms of the chair. Unbelievable. Her voice quivered. "Yes. My brother's girlfriend, Elle."

Grateful the officer placed the photo of Elle at the plantation house back into the folder, Lei's mind whirled. So did Kimo lie to her regarding Elle's trip to the house when he said she hadn't left home all day? Why would he do it? What would he have to gain? Had Elle snuck out without his knowledge? And what did she want?

"Miss Hudson, I'll need some additional information about Elle, if you happen to know the answers. Elle doesn't know the address of the residence where she lives in Kahului, or so she states."

"It's a friend of the family, Dirk Carrington. I'll give you his business card with the information. Elle's from Oahu and hasn't been here long. I don't know her well, but I'm surprised she would do this."

"Elle doesn't have a prior record, but now she's charged with breaking and entering. Luckily your neighbor caught sight of her and called right away. For the record, did you notice anything missing?"

"No." She hadn't scrutinized the entire house, but she had little worth stealing besides the old TV, laptop and sewing machine which remained there. "What will happen to her now?"

"She'll appear before a judge. I can't say for sure. It's an offense, but with no prior record she'll likely get fined, maybe sentenced with some community service."

"Thank you." She stood and shook the officer's hand.

Acid churned in her stomach as she headed to the car and called her sister.

"I'm in town, Malia. Mind if I stop by? I've got some unpleasant news."

"It wouldn't concern Elle, would it?"

Her voice grew loud. "How did you know?"

"Kimo called a few minutes ago. He's coming over. Why don't you join us?"

"I'll be there in a few minutes." She left the police station, zipped along the highway and turned onto the dusty road toward Malia's apartment. Doing the best to avoid the potholes, she pulled into the driveway. Clouds of red dust settled after the vehicle came to a halt.

Lei stepped out of the car into the intense summer heat. It didn't take long for the humid air to make clothes stick to a person, in addition to the stress she endured.

No sign of Kimo's new, red car yet. She marched to the door.

Malia opened it. "Sorry about the break-in at your house. What was Elle thinking?"

"I can't for the life of me imagine." She followed Malia into the compact living room where they sat. She dropped her purse on the worn sofa beside her. "Why didn't she call me and come over rather than break a window? It makes no sense. Elle didn't have a record. Now she does."

"Crazy. I have no idea." Malia wrinkled her nose. "Maybe Kimo will have some thoughts."

"Oh, I'm sure he will." Lei crossed her arms and grasped her elbows. She swallowed hard. "Elle came looking around the property a while ago. My neighbor's description of the person fit Elle, so I called Kimo to see if she'd stopped by when I wasn't home. Kimo said she didn't and had been home all day with him.

Now, seeing Elle again today, my neighbor confirmed her as the same person who came to my house a while ago when I wasn't home."

With eyes wide, Malia moved forward. "Whoa."

"Did he lie to me, Malia? Or lie for Elle? Or did she disappear while Kimo thought she was home?"

"Who knows? What is up with them?" Malia threw her head back and blew out a breath. "This is too weird."

"Yeah, tell me about it. I can't wait to hear what Kimo says about Elle's actions." She fidgeted on the couch and clasped the purse to her side.

The doorbell rang.

Malia rose. "I'll get it."

Kimo swaggered in, took a seat in a chair beside Malia and stared at Lei. "What a day."

Lei wanted to scream. "For sure. You don't know the half of it."

Malia pressed her hands along her thighs and straightened out the creases in her Capri pants. "Do you want to talk about it, Kimo?"

"Not so much. I'm upset since it will cost a lot of money. Elle doesn't have any and I've spent a lot on my car. I'll need some financial help to bail her out of this."

Lei wanted to ask him the definition of "this" namely the break-in to her house, which he conveniently left out of his statement. Her brows rushed together and her eyes narrowed. "Without cash, she'll probably have to stay in jail, I would imagine."

His voice bellowed. "Are you insane? I had to listen to Elle whine half the day today. I'm not putting up with it forever." Kimo turned toward Malia. "Can you give me some money?"

Malia glanced at her, then back at Kimo. "How much are we talking about? I've paid some school bills and will have more to pay, plus I've invested some of my money and I can't easily withdraw it without penalties."

He looked downward and rubbed a brow. "Not sure what it'll cost yet, but I'll let you know." Kimo caught Lei's gaze. "I suppose you won't volunteer either."

Lei's facial muscles tensed as she pursed her lips. "Let's see. In the first place, I don't have excess cash. Second, I'm starting a new business, barely making ends meet." Her voice thundered. "Third, I don't see why I should pay for Elle's mistake, when she broke into my home."

Cheeks red, he adopted a challenging tone. "I figured you'd bring it up and throw it in my face. I'm sorry, Lei, but I'm not the one who did it. Remember, it's only a window."

Her stomach roiled. "Kimo. It's not only about a broken window. Elle committed a crime and has a record now. And for what? I told you more than once she's welcome to come visit. Why did she do it? What does she want?"

Kimo shook his head, his voice softer. "How would I know?"

"You're the most familiar with her. She was the one who came onto my property before when I called and asked you if she'd come to visit. You said she hadn't left the house all day. What's going on here?"

"I don't remember saying anything about her whereabouts to you." He turned his head to the side.

"Of course, you don't." She took in some shallow breaths. Talking with Kimo got her nowhere. What did she expect? Elle was his girlfriend.

Kimo lowered his head. "Maybe I thought she was home and she wasn't, okay?"

"Have you thought about calling Elle's parents, Kimo?" Malia fidgeted with her T-shirt, twisting the bottom of it in her hand. "Maybe she should go back home to Oahu."

"No, I haven't called them. I doubt they'll help either."

Lei's shoulders dropped, and her arms hung heavy at her sides. "This is upsetting for all of us, but it's sad, too. I'd hoped for much better for you and Elle."

He clasped his hands and stared at his feet. "Whatever. If you don't have the cash, fine. Don't concern yourself with our lives. Maybe Dirk will help us. I wish we had more family support and help, but then again, we never did. I've gotta go."

Malia's voice wavered. "Good-bye, Kimo."

Tires squealed and a cloud of dust whirled in front of the living room, shaking the window.

Jaw clenched, Lei's nails dug into her palms. "Did I make a mistake with all I said, Malia? Elle has to learn to take responsibility for her actions, but I feel bad about it, too. Kimo is our brother. I know they haven't had easy lives and everyone makes mistakes."

"No, I think what you said worked well. He needs to realize the path Elle's dealing with now, and if he has any part in it, to rethink his future. But of course, he tried to smooth over any wrongdoing to you. Maybe he'll think it over now."

"Thanks. You make me feel better. I don't seem able to help anyone else like I should, while others help me. If it wasn't for you and Jess today and my neighbor, Mrs. Chen, I don't know what I would've done."

Malia came to her side and squeezed her shoulder. "You've helped me and others more than you know. Kimo and I looked up to you when life fell apart at home. You're not used to receiving, only giving, and you deserve some happiness now." She pulled back. "Except on certain days, I guess."

"Yeah, it's life." Lei offered a bemused grin and leaned her head against Malia's arm.

"For sure." Malia returned to her seat. "Do you want to stay for dinner?"

"No, my window's supposed to get installed and I should go home and do some sewing. Let's get together again soon."

She drove back to Lahaina thankful for Malia, Tutu and Jess, and she'd pray for Kimo and Elle.

Maybe she'd consider visiting Elle if she remained at the correction center for another day or so. Pastor Kane volunteered for jail ministry and visits, too. She'd call him tomorrow.

When Lei turned into her driveway, she gazed at the new window. What a relief she didn't have to deal with it herself. Later, she'd thank Jess and Mrs. Chen.

Exiting the car, she turned. A rustle at the hibiscus bushes caught her attention. Jess passed through. "I heard your car. Everything turn out all right?"

Her pulse rose as she raced into his arms. "It is now. I can't thank you enough."

Jess smoothed her hair back, gazed into her eyes and kissed her long and slow.

Lei didn't want the kiss to end, but knew she should pull back.

After relaying the information to him, she entered the house and flipped on the kitchen light. Home at last. She cherished the word "home" more than ever. A feeling of comfort and stability for now. Would it stay that way?

Jess's past comments came to mind. He'd stated things would get better. Yes, hope and faith helped.

CHAPTER EIGHT

The next afternoon after visiting Tutu, Lei entered the correction center. Guided to a chair in front of a glass window, Lei waited. Elle sauntered into the room on the other side of the glass, glanced away and slid into the seat, shoulders slumped.

"I didn't come to berate you, Elle. I only want to understand why you didn't come to see me, if you wanted to come into the house."

Elle chewed the nail on her index finger and gazed at Lei. "It wasn't about coming to visit you at the house."

Her head flinched back. What did she mean? "Would you please to tell me what the reason was? Maybe I can help you with whatever it is."

Elle fiddled with the end of one of her shirtsleeves. "I don't suppose it matters now."

"What doesn't matter? Tell me." Her spine rigid, she tapped her fingers on her thigh, and wondered which one of the two of them were the most nervous.

"I'm not supposed to say." With slouched posture, Elle's chin dipped to her chest.

So she protected someone. Kimo, of course. "Remember Kimo's my brother and I love him. I told you I'm not here to place blame. What's in the house you think is so important?"

Elle lowered her gaze, her voice soft. "Fishhooks."

Lei squinted. She didn't fish. "What fishhooks? I don't have any."

"We heard you had them. Some expensive ones. Kimo's running out of money. I thought if I could get them for him, it would help. I'd do anything for him. But he didn't know I went looking for them."

Lei shook her head. Unfortunately, it cost Elle more than she understood. "Getting a police record isn't worth it. I hope you realize it now." She drew in a breath and touched a fingertip to her lips. It dawned on her. The fishhook collection Dirk mentioned at Tutu's home during the meeting when they received their inheritances from Tutu's deceased husband, Henry.

Dirk had mentioned *maka'u*, a nice collection of old Hawaiian fishhooks his Great Uncle Henry had collected and wondered what had happened to them. Some were made of koa, jade, abalone, mother-of-pearl, and even fossil ivory he'd said. "I thought they were in my grandmother's home. She even offered to look for them before she moved into assisted living."

"Kimo said they weren't there. Henry's family owned the plantation house before you moved into it."

She squeezed her eyes shut and pinched the skin between her brows. Kimo had mentioned relics when he'd first visited her. "For heaven's sake, I'll look for them."

With a distant gaze, Elle nodded.

"When can you leave the facility?"

"Dirk's coming to collect me tomorrow."

Lei stood. "Nice of him. I'm sorry this trip hasn't turned out good for you. Thanks for answering my question. Now I understand."

She returned home. What a pleasant surprise to see Jess in his yard waving at her after the stressful visit with Elle.

Jess whipped through the hibiscus bushes. "You know if we keep this up, we will have a permanent path between our houses."

The warmth from his hug and his sense of humor made her relax. "It works for me."

"Why don't you come over? I'll order some Chinese takeout and we can talk."

"It's a deal." Her fortress of strength. But for how long?

At his house, Lei sat at the kitchen table, which sported the tapa tablecloth she'd made for him. While he ordered the takeout, she glanced around the kitchen and living area. A few new rugs, along with the chair slipcovers she'd sewn for him, Jess had made the house his own. But something was missing.

"They'll deliver it." Jess joined her at the table.

"Great. You've made the place homier, but I noticed you don't have your laptop out here as usual."

Jess stretched his legs out under the table. "Yeah. I keep it in the bedroom now."

"No more genealogy or DNA?" How surprising, since he'd been so adamant about it.

"No. Not for the time being. And I use my phone for most of my social media, anyway."

"Me, too."

He leaned forward. "Do you want to share anymore about the break-in? I'm hoping it's settled."

She relayed the information Kimo's girlfriend offered regarding the fishhooks. "Can you believe it? Maʻkua. Fishhooks, of all things."

"Young people don't consider the possible consequences when they do things. But some of those old fishhooks are worth a lot."

Lei tilted her head toward the ceiling and let out a heavy sigh. "I haven't found any in the house, but I'll go through every corner and closet tomorrow and let Kimo know. With any luck it might calm them for a while."

"One can hope." Jess scratched his chin. "Have you noticed any more tracks or disturbances in the backyard since the incident with the digging?"

"No, thank heavens. But it continues to stump me."

A rap on the kitchen door compelled Jess to stand. "It's probably the delivery guy."

With the cupboard doors open, Lei grabbed two plates for them.

Jess set the white, square cardboard containers on the table. "Help yourself. There's chicken, beef and a pork dish with rice." He tossed her some packaged chopsticks. They filled their plates and ate.

"Have you heard any more about how much longer you might continue your employment at the hotel?" Lei hated to think of Jess leaving. When did she become so attached to him?

Chopsticks in his hand, Jess stopped eating. "No. Nothing's changed. They haven't asked me to stay on any longer than originally planned."

Her shoulders dropped, and she gazed downward. "Oh. I hoped they would."

"I'll ask next time I'm at work."

"What will you do if they don't extend the job and you haven't received any notification from the investigation position you want? Will you stay here on the island?"

Finished eating, he pushed his chair back, huffed out a breath and cracked his knuckles. "I originally thought I'd try to pick up something temporary on Oahu when my current job is finished here. But yeah, I hope to stay here now. There are a few places I can apply around here, but the pay won't be as good as what I'm getting at the hotel. I can get by for a while."

"I'm glad to hear it. I've enjoyed your friendship and appreciated your help, of course." Lei sucked in a quick breath. She'd never admitted her feelings so bluntly to anyone.

"I feel the same. You're the main reason I'd like to stay here as long as I can afford it."

Breathless, her heart hammered. What was happening between them? In the end, they had different pathways to follow in their lives. She stammered. "I should go. I can't ever get too far ahead with my sewing inventory. The new purses are practically jumping off the sale table."

"Wait. Please. I hoped we could walk over to the ocean. It's such a nice evening. Just for a little while."

"I don't know." She wanted to, yet debated. Could she face more loss again, since he would eventually leave?

Jess put his arm around her and touched her lip with his index finger. "Please, for me."

"Okay." She melted at his touch.

Hand in hand they walked across the yard, crossed Front Street and continued to the lava rock retaining wall in front of the sand and ocean beyond. The trade winds blew Lei's hair. They sat on the edge of the wall. The waves came in, their rhythmic motion soothing.

Searching the sky, Jess pointed. "I see the constellation Scorpio, or as it's known here, Maui's fishhook, if I remember right."

"Yeah, you have to admit the hook, or the scorpion tail sits perfectly on top of the ocean at this vantage point, as if it's ready to catch some fish."

"Yup, exactly." Jess placed his arm around her shoulder and gazed into her eyes. "We talked a while ago about my work and where I might go. Would you ever consider living anywhere else?"

A shiver ran up her spine. "I don't think so. Maui's my home, my stability. Regardless of whatever else happens in my life, the connection with the land remains. It's sacred to us Hawaiians. And it's what I know and love, next to God, of course."

"Could you find it possible to trust me in such a way?" Jess smoothed back the flying strands of hair from her face.

"I honestly don't know." Lei trembled from his touch, but maintained strong eye contact. "This is all new to me. I've never considered it before and haven't had the opportunity."

Jess pulled her close, his voice soft. "There's a first time for everything." His lips touched hers and she melted into him.

Breathless and light-headed, she pulled back and faced the ocean. The cell phone vibrated, and she dug in her pocket. Malia. "Do you mind if I take this Jess? It's my sister."

"Of course, not. Go ahead."

Lei turned her head. "What is it Malia?"

"There's been an accident."

Her voice intensified. "Tell me who."

"Kimo. He drove into a parked car. I don't know yet if he'll go to the hospital, or the circumstances other than what I've told you. I'll call you back later when I find out more."

Lei jerked her head back. Would he be all right? She faced Jess. "It's my brother. He's had a car accident."

"Is he okay?"

"Malia wasn't sure if they'd take him to the hospital yet, so I'm hoping it means he isn't badly hurt."

"Anything I can do?"

She sat upright, her spine rigid. "No. Malia will call me when she knows the details. I need to return to the house. We'll talk again another time. It's been wonderful sitting out here with you tonight, but the real world is calling again."

*

The next afternoon Lei waited in the correction center again, waiting in the lobby for Malia to finish her visit with Kimo.

The rigid, uncomfortable seat hit every bone and muscle in the wrong place as she squirmed around. She had no idea what to say to Kimo, but needed to see him. She hadn't known how to answer Jess last night either, and didn't now, even after a day to mull his comments over.

Why did he care if she lived on Maui or not? Did he only want to see if she could change her life? Or maybe considered her too rigid or narrow-minded? He'd lived on the mainland, Oahu and Maui. She leaned back into the hard, plastic chair connected to the wall.

The question of most concern, trusting Jess, had set her off in a tailspin. Lei wanted to trust him, but wasn't sure if she could or should. Perhaps after getting to know him better or spending more time with him? Hard to say.

Difficult as the situations were with Elle and Kimo, she could cope and relate easier since they fit the pattern in her life, family problems. But her relationship with Jess didn't.

High heels clicked on the tile floor and Lei turned. Malia walked toward her.

"Hi. Kimo's in a good mood today. I think this accident definitely shook him. Hopefully it'll make him grow up. I'm thankful he wasn't hurt, but Kimo landed in jail for not fully cooperating with the police after the accident and stating he wanted to leave."

"Let's hope he's learned from this." Lei stood and hugged her sister. "Will they release him soon?"

"Yes. Let me know how your visit goes. I'm going home and change out of these clothes and into something comfortable."

"Understood. I'll talk to you later."

Lei asked the attendant for a visit with Kimo. She followed the man through the hallway and into a small room. Kimo sat in a chair and stared into the distance until she took a seat in front of him.

"Hi Kimo. Glad you're all right."

He scratched his head. "Yeah, I know I could've gotten hurt and stuff."

"You have insurance, thank heavens."

"Yeah, but the insurance will go sky high now. It was high enough before, since I'm male and a young age."

She dragged a hand through her hair, thankful he understood some of the consequences of his actions. "You've got time to decide what you want to do about the car once it's repaired."

Jaw clenched, beads of sweat covered his forehead. "Malia said Elle is upset."

"It's understandable. She cares about you, more than you might think."

"What do you mean?" He squinted and cocked his head to the side.

"Elle was willing to do most anything to find those supposed fishhooks for you. She told me when I visited her here recently."

A vein in his neck engorged and his tone deepened. "Go ahead. Let me have it." He clenched his fists and stared at her.

"No, Kimo, I'm not. Elle told me she wanted to help you in any way since she cares about you. I thought you should know. I'll try to reach her later and see how she's doing."

He sat upright. "Look, I'm jumpy today, all right?"

"Of course. I understand. I also want to make you aware I checked closets, old boxes and the whole house this morning. After searching everywhere, I didn't find any fishhooks."

His eyes searched hers. "You don't have to say nice stuff to me since I'm in here."

Shoulders pulled back, she stared at him. "I meant what I said."

After a brief knock on the door, a guard entered and faced Kimo. "Pastor Puʻa Kane has arrived to see you."

Kimo raised his head. "All right, send him in, please."

Lei turned toward the man. "Sir, can I stay if it's okay with my brother and the pastor?"

The guard nodded at her and left the room.

"Kimo, do you mind if I stay for a while?" She drew in a breath. "He's the pastor at my new church."

"Sure, why not? I don't have anything better to do, so you might as well stick around, too."

The guard brought in another chair, followed by Pastor Kane carrying his Bible. "Aloha, Lei." He turned and sat in the chair. "And this must be Kimo."

"Yes, sir." He gazed at Pastor Kane.

"Pastor, I'm here since Kimo is my brother."

His eyes widened. "Oh. Okay." The pastor removed his Bible from the case.

"Pastor, I hope you'll pray for me." Kimo folded his hands.

The pastor scratched his gray beard. "I'll tell you what I say to all the people I visit here. They ask me to pray for them. And I say, I did pray for you. It's why you're here now, alive, in place of what might have been. It's a second chance to change your ways and your life. Most of the time people don't stop to think landing in jail is a blessing of sorts."

Kimo's eyes narrowed and he leaned forward. "What? I sure didn't think so."

The pastor clutched his Bible in one hand. "When people come here, it's often a wake-up call to turn their life around, help themselves or let others help them find the right path back to a better life."

He lowered his head, his voice softer. "Oh. Yeah, I suppose."

Pastor Kane pointed his index finger straight upward. "We have to surrender to God what keeps us away from him. For some, it's drug addictions, as an example. There are many such crutches for people. At first, it appears as an easier way to cope rather than giving everything to God. But in the end it never works."

Lei loved the land. It certainly wasn't an addiction, but did it keep her away from God when she should've focused on Him? Her homeland remained when people didn't and gave her comfort when others couldn't. But what about focusing on God only? A tall order, but worth pondering.

"Don't take my word for it, Kimo." He opened his tattered Bible. "Proverbs 16:3. 'Commit to the Lord, whatever you do, and He will establish your plans.'" Pastor licked his forefinger and thumbed a few pages ahead. "Proverbs 16:9. 'In their hearts humans plan their course, but the Lord establishes their steps.'"

"Cool." He raised an eyebrow.

She agreed. Once again Pastor Kane gave her something to think about. She hoped Kimo took it to heart, too. Thankfully, he'd never had a problem believing in the Lord.

Pastor tucked his Bible away in its case. "We can talk over anything you want, Kimo. Then we'll pray, all right?"

"Yeah, okay."

Lei took the cue to leave. "Take care, Kimo and see you soon." She turned and faced the pastor. "Thanks for coming. I'll see you on Sunday at the hotel, if not before then."

He nodded and smiled back at her.

Lei left them and walked back to the lobby area to give Malia a quick call. She grabbed the phone and punched in the number. Several rings later, the call shifted to voicemail.

"Malia, I've finished my visit with Kimo. You're right. He's doing well. I thought I'd stop by before returning to Lahaina. I'll try you again before coming to your apartment."

After a call to Jess, she also spoke with Tutu and Dirk about her visit with Kimo. Dirk and Tutu hadn't heard anything from Malia after her visit with Kimo. Fifteen minutes had passed since the first call. She grabbed the phone and called Malia. Again, Malia's phone rang until voicemail answered. Maybe she'd taken a shower or ran to the store. "I've decided to drive to your apartment, Malia. If you're not home by the time I get there, we'll connect later."

Dashing through the darkness and heavy rain into the parking lot, she hopped in the car. Storms often rolled in quick, but this one came on full force. With the wipers thumping on double speed, she headed toward Malia's apartment. The rain poured down, and only car headlights shone through the torrents.

The road near the apartment she turned on had now become a mud bath as the car sloshed along. A tow truck hauling Malia's smashed car came into view.

Her heart hammered in her chest. She gasped for air, but it wouldn't come. *Please God, let Malia be all right.* She wheezed, got out of the car and ran up to the man sitting in the truck. He lowered the window partway.

Wet and shaky, she leaned against the door and gripped the window's edge. "This is my sister's car. What happened? Where is she?"

"I don't know the details. I got a call to haul this car away. The cops were here earlier. You might want to check the hospital, by the looks of this vehicle."

The hospital. Rain poured over her face, washing her tears with it.

Inside the car, she shook, looked up the hospital number on her phone and made the call.

"Maui Memorial Medical Center. How may I help you?"

"I'd like you to check if my sister, Malia Hudson is a patient."

"One moment, please." Music played through phone. "No, we don't have a Malia Hudson listed."

"How about Jenny Taylor or Sara Watts?" With breathing more labored, she fidgeted. She continued driving to Malia's apartment and parked while the blasted music continued on the phone. The apartment was dark. Where were Malia's roommates?

"We do have a Jenny Taylor registered."

"Thank you."

She pulled out and headed toward the hospital. What happened to Jenny and why was Malia's car crashed?

Twenty minutes later, Lei sprinted through sheets of rain hammering the parking lot at the hospital. She pushed through the revolving door of the emergency department and shook out her rain jacket. In the corner of the waiting area sat Malia, her head in her hands, sobbing.

A hand flew to Lei's chest, and she rushed to her sister's side. "Malia. Are you all right?"

Malia's head jerked up, and she stood. "Thank heavens you're here. Jenny was in an awful accident with my car."

Lei hugged her. "Shh. I'm here to stay with you now. Is Jenny going to be okay?"

"I don't know." Malia rubbed her forehead.

"Come, let's sit down and you can tell me what happened."

In the corner of the waiting area, Malia's hands shook, and she drew in a breath. "Jenny's car stalled at work so she called someone to check out the problem and got a ride home with a co-worker in the meantime. Sara's out of town, but Jenny needed to attend a class, so I let her borrow my car. A few minutes after she left the apartment, I heard a loud crash. I called the police and told them, in case no one else did. I looked out the door, but couldn't see anything. It was raining so hard."

"Oh, Malia. How awful." Lei pushed Malia's bangs out of her eyes.

"It was my car. Mine. It worked fine for me earlier today."

"How do you know it didn't drive well for Jenny? How did the accident happen?"

Malia blew her nose and faced her sister. "Jenny was conscious when I first saw her. She told me she tried to stop before turning onto the highway and the brakes didn't work, so the car crashed into a van. I found out later the people in the van were all okay, but Jenny's in surgery now and has lots of injuries. Her parents are waiting with her. They will stay all night and said they'd take it from here. The police called me since the car's in my name and they came to the apartment to speak with me. I gave them what little information I had, and they brought me to the hospital to be with her."

An orderly passed through the doors wheeling an empty cart, and a group of people dripping wet entered through the revolving door and headed to the reception area.

Lei had to be strong for Malia. "I can take you home, or better yet come to my house tonight. I tried to reach you earlier after visiting Kimo, but your phone switched to voicemail. When I arrived at the apartment to see if you were home, I passed the wrecker truck on the way."

Malia bolted upright and dug into her purse. "Oh. I forgot to turn my phone back on. They requested it stay off when I was in the emergency room with Jenny before her parents came." She turned the phone on and put it away. "I should go home. I have to work tomorrow and can get a ride with someone."

"Are you sure?" She took Malia's hand in hers, wishing she could do something more for her. Anything.

"Yeah. My other roommate, Sara, will return home in the morning. Besides, the police want to keep in touch with me due to the circumstances of the accident."

It didn't sound good. What was going on? "You mean since Jenny said the brakes were at fault?"

"I'm sure it's part of the reason."

"Are you saying they think someone tampered with the car?" The thought certainly occurred to Lei.

"It's a possibility. And I'm the owner of the vehicle."

Lei tugged at her collar and her skin tingled where perspiration formed on her neck. "It would mean someone would've had to meddle with the car brakes after you got home from work I would think, unless it takes a while for them to break all the way through."

"I suppose. It got dark before the rainstorm. Jenny and I had an early supper since she had class. We didn't hear anything, and we can't see out the window at the area where we park the car, of course. So I have no idea where or when it could've happened. Maybe something else caused it."

Hands clammy, Lei's leg muscles tightened, and she flinched when the reception desk phone rang. A sick feeling roiled in her gut. The whole incident sounded fishy to her. But who would do something like this? She didn't even want to imagine. "Did the police ask you who might've had reason to do such a thing?"

Malia looked downward. "Yeah, in case they find something wrong with the car. They said they'll look at the vehicle before any repair work is done on it, if it's fixable."

She surveyed her sister's face. "What did you tell them?"

A siren rang as an emergency vehicle pulled into the garage outside.

Perspiration formed on Malia's upper lip and she glanced everywhere but at Lei. She spoke in a hushed tone. "I didn't tell them anything."

She gasped. "Oh, Malia. You must tell them about the history with Eric, or I will. It's not likely, but you never know."

Malia lowered her head. "Let's see what they have to say when they call me back."

"I'll talk to Jess and see what he recommends for security for you at the apartment. This is downright frightening, especially if the brakes were cut." She sat upright to ease her aching back.

Malia's bottom lip and chin quivered. "I don't know what to think. Everything's falling apart. Poor Jenny. Kimo called Tutu, and she's upset about his accident. I would imagine Dirk's fed up with both Kimo and Elle and their problems. You've had someone digging around your house, of all things. It's crazy."

"Malia, listen to me." Lei took Malia by the shoulders and tightened her grip. "You're coming home with me tonight. I'll bring you back early in the morning before work. I can take you to rent a car then, or someone can take you to get one later on after work. We'll see what the police say and go from there. I'm sure Jenny's parents will call you once surgery is over or if there are any major changes."

"Yeah, you're right." Malia stood.

After fumbling for the car keys in her purse, Lei put on the wet rain jacket.

The cell phone buzzed and her sister grabbed it from her purse. "Hello? Yes, this is Malia Hudson." She turned and her gaze flickered back and forth. "Oh no. Thanks for the information. Yes, I'll come in tomorrow." Eerily calm, Malia ended the call and stared out the window.

Lei wanted to jump through the windowpane. "What did they say?"

A dazed look crept over Malia's face. "they're certain someone tampered with the brake lines."

CHAPTER NINE

The next morning, Jess finished his first cup of coffee, thankful Lei's brother wasn't hurt. He'd check in with her again if he didn't hear from her soon.

Arms stretched above his head, he waited for the strong Kona brew to help jolt him awake. At the kitchen counter, he poured himself another steaming, cup. The aroma infused his nostrils and sometimes even rivaled the taste.

A glance at the small, kitchen cabinet drawer drew his attention. It's where he'd last stashed the plastic-covered photo. He pulled it out and returned to the table. Taking a sip of coffee, he held the precious picture in front of him. The beautiful baby girl in the basinet at the hospital nursery. He'd taken the snapshot through the glass and watched the baby move her tiny fingers and cry before the nurse took her away. His index finger brushed over the baby's image. Every detail of the wonderful memory remained intact.

With shoulders dropped and his spine bowed, he clutched the picture in his hand and studied it a little longer. Wrapped in a pink blanket with a tiny hat on, he couldn't see much of the baby's face. Did she look like Paula now? He squeezed his eyes shut to hold back the sting of tears.

Jess bit his lip, took in a deep breath and placed the photograph back in the drawer. For the first time in quite a while, he'd opened his laptop early this morning in preparation for searching the Jules family later. A certainty regarding the child's biological father, not only for himself and his mother, but to have definite answers for Lei, would put him at ease. To know the truth and have concrete facts helped urge him on, especially since he and Lei had become closer.

Back at the table, his conversation with her at the beach swept through his mind. He'd asked her to trust in him. Was not revealing his strong possibility of fatherhood dishonest? But what if he never found Paula and her daughter?

Also, as stated by his mother, he shouldn't make comments or claims if they consisted of assumptions and unproven statements. What if he told Lei he thought he had a child, made a big deal out of it, but later on couldn't find the youngster, let alone prove it? In any case, he hadn't succeeded in the last seven years.

Jess swallowed more coffee. He'd become more serious about his relationship with Lei. If she returned his feelings and wanted to continue their relationship, maybe he should tell her, regardless of the unanswered questions about Paula's child. It gave him good reason to check on the Internet again, didn't it? Yet he admitted seeing the print of the baby girl again motivated him even more. If she was his child, she deserved a father.

With his cup empty again, he poured himself the last of the coffee and returned to the table. The phone call from Malia had interrupted his conversation with Lei while at the ocean. He drummed his fingers on the table. Yes, he'd gear up for a serious discussion with her soon. Whether or not he uncovered the truth from his past, they could share their feelings for each other.

The screen door rattled from a few raps on it. "It's Lei."

Jess grinned, leaned forward and tipped his head toward the door. "Come in."

As gorgeous as ever, she seated herself at the kitchen table next to him.

His pulse increased. "To what do I owe this pleasant morning visit?"

She stared downward at the table, her gaze distant. "A couple of things. First, on a lighter note, I wanted to let you know I've been thinking more about looking for my father since we talked about it." She raised her head and gazed at him. "He's a big part of the reason I have trouble with my past. You helped me realize I might have some closure if I knew what became of him, whether it's pleasant news or not. I'm ready for your help to get started."

The information brought a smile to his face. "I'm glad to hear it. My gut feeling is you won't be sorry. Then you can deal with it and go on from there."

"Malia is in full agreement with the idea, too." She scooted her chair forward and paused. "Jess, I hope you don't mind. I want to ask you about a security question again."

A security issue would explain her serious demeanor. His brows drew together. "Is everything okay? What's happened now?"

Lei huffed out a breath. "Long story short, my sister's car brakes were severed, her roommate happened to be driving the car and is in serious condition from an accident."

His mouth fell open. "Oh, no. I'm sorry. How terrible." He placed his hand on her forearm. "You should've called me. What can I do to help?"

"I took Malia back to her apartment this morning since another one of her roommates will return and she won't be there alone. They'll talk to the landlord about security, but I wondered if you have any ideas for what they might do to protect themselves on their own and make them feel a little safer."

Elbows on the table, he propped his fists against his cheeks. "For starters, they should replace their porch light with a motion detector and go out together at night only when necessary, if possible. Carry pepper spray. Can they see their cars from the apartment?"

"No, I'm afraid not and there aren't any garages." Lei stared downward, and her voice wavered. "Malia's most upset about her roommate. I'm worried sick for both of them."

Jess dashed to her side and hugged her. "Of course, you are. I can drive to Kahului and take a look around the apartment area if you want."

She exhaled and looked up at him. "Do you think it might help?"

"I don't know, but it can't hurt. What do the police say?" He smoothed her hair back in hopes to calm her.

Her voice trembled. "It's an intentional act and since it happened to Malia's car, she may have been the target."

"Wow. Scary, for sure." Adrenaline poured through him. "Tell you what. After work, I'll drive there and take a look. Maybe I'll get a few more ideas once I see the apartment and property. Give Malia a call and let her know I'll drive there this afternoon so she's aware I'm coming and what I plan to do." He returned to his chair at the table.

She pulled a notepad and pen from her purse, jotted down the address and handed it to Jess. "Thanks. It means a lot. Sorry to dump this on you, but I trust you when it comes to incidents like this. You've been a great help to me."

She trusted him, even if only for his skills. "No problem at all. It's my thing. I'm glad to help if I can."

"The placemats and table cloth you ordered for your mother are my gift in return."

"Not necessary, but thank you. I appreciate it." He stroked her forearm.

"I should get going." Lei stood. "I see you have your laptop open. I'm sure you have things to do, too."

"Yeah. I'll look at it later. I'm doing a search now and then, hoping to complete something."

She tipped her head. "Sounds mysterious. I don't understand. For work?"

A chance to speak the truth. But they both had work this morning and Lei had enough to deal with for the moment. "I suppose it does sound odd." He bit at his bottom lip, and his eye twitched. "It's not for work. It's personal. Something I need resolved from the past."

As she stared at him, her body stiffened and her voice became flat. "I see. Then I won't keep you. Have a good day." She turned toward the door.

Lei had shared the search regarding her father, but he'd clammed up about his own search. He rushed toward her and squeezed her shoulder. "Wait. I want to tell you. I'd hoped to have it settled before now. Then I'd have the facts to discuss it without my questions looming, but it hasn't happened so far. So I'll tell you what I do know, talk to you tonight and fill you in on what I find at Malia's, too. Come for dinner around six o'clock. Then we'll talk. Okay?"

"You are a hard man to turn down, Jess, but I'm not sure." She sighed.

"What you think matters to me." He'd scared her and could sense her pulling away like a snail in its shell.

"All right. I'll listen to what you have to say. Good-bye." The screen door clicked shut.

Clearing up an issue from the past could've been anything. Jess squeezed his eyes shut a moment and took in a few shallow breaths. He hadn't explained himself correctly. For all she knew, he could be a serial killer on the run. Fool.

He moved the laptop in front of him on the table. Might as well have a look, after what he'd said during Lei's visit.

Fingers tapped at the keyboard as Jess ran a search on John Jules. He munched on one of Mrs. Chen's malasadas and sipped his Kona brew while the search engine gathered the information. Scrolling down the list of matches, he found many of the usual Jules listed not connected with Paula.

He jerked back from the table, eyes wide, and his jaw slacked open. Could it be? He pointed the mouse and double-clicked on a new entry he hadn't found before in his searching. Correct name, reasonable age and the area where they lived. A surge of energy gushed through his body and his heart boomed in his chest. Breathless, he continued reading. John Jules had passed away, survived by his daughter, Paula and granddaughter, Eva Rose.

A mad dash from his chair knocked his coffee cup from the table with a crash to the floor. Never mind, he had to pull the photo from the drawer. Jess blinked repeatedly and his hand shook as he rubbed his thumb over the photo. After all these years, a name to connect with the baby girl. Eva Rose. His lower lip quivered and his thoughts scrambled. He wanted to glean more information if possible, but the clock on the kitchen wall indicated work started soon.

While sorry for Paula, Eva Rose and the family for their loss, Jess couldn't help but hope to find the answers and the closure he needed so much.

After picking up the fragments of the broken mug, he stashed the photo away and headed to the bedroom to dress in his uniform.

Since he'd waited this long, he could wait a little longer, but his thoughts rushed ahead full speed. If Eva Rose was his daughter, could he get to know her? Would she want to meet him? What about Paula's thoughts on the matter? And also concerning to him, what about Lei? He was on shaky ground with her right now. One thing for sure, he would tell her the truth about his new finding.

Unable to believe his discovery, Jess raced out of the house toward the car. He took a deep breath to get his head together, focus on work and for his trip to Malia's apartment later. And hope for the best when he met with Lei tonight.

CHAPTER TEN

In the evening after dinner, Lei rinsed her plate in Jess's kitchen sink.

Jess pushed his chair back from the table. "I hope some of my suggestions for Malia's security will help. I had a chance to talk to the landlord. He seemed like a nice enough guy." His words rushed out. "It sounds like he might agree to installing a camera facing out to view the parked cars in addition to the motion detector I suggested. As long as she isn't living alone, it's some comfort, too."

Palms together, Lei gazed upward for a moment. "Yes, I hope so." She grabbed Jess's plate, rinsed it off and placed it in the dishwasher along with her own. He'd talked fast and furious since she'd arrived. Maybe what he had to say regarding his past made him nervous. She wouldn't bring up the subject unless he did. And if he didn't, it likely meant he didn't care enough to trust her with the information. In case, she would brace herself for the worst of disappointments. They'd had a good run and a better relationship than she could have ever imagined in the short amount of time they'd spent together.

She cleared the rest of the table, wiped it off and sat across from Jess. "Malia's friend isn't out of danger yet, the poor girl."

"It's sad." He leaned closer to her. "What about Eric? Any news?"

Lips pressed together, she raised her brows. "Supposedly he was away on a trip to Oahu. It doesn't mean he couldn't have hired someone to rig the brakes, according to the police. On the other hand, we haven't heard anything from Eric in quite a while. Not a word since he showed up saying he didn't want Malia around. And so it brings us back to who else is possibly responsible for the accident and why it happened. They're leaving all options open yet. I don't know what to think."

He poked his tongue into his cheek. "It's hard to figure out without any idea for a motive. Let's hope it gets resolved soon."

"For sure. Malia and Jenny didn't deserve this. They're both kind, gentle people." Lei folded her hands over the table and looked downward. She would leave in a few minutes if Jess didn't want to open up and share more with her. "I'll have your mother's order finished by the end of the week. I'll drop it by when it's completed."

"Oh, thanks. Take your time. I know she'll love the Hawaiian, hand-sewn items." Jess rubbed his forehead.

She gazed around the kitchen and living area. The tablecloth she'd made for Jess sat folded over one of the kitchen chairs while they'd eaten. The tan and gray slipcovers graced the living room chairs. Teeth pinched at her bottom lip as she remembered how good he'd been to her. A heaviness seeped through her body. "Dinner was delicious. You've had a long day, Jess. Maybe you'd like some down time. If so, I can get ready to leave anytime."

"No, please stay." He extended his arm. "Would you like to go into the living room so we can talk?"

The request to go into the living room might signal something serious. "Right here is fine, and then I'll head out." She fidgeted and wet her lips.

Jess scratched his chin. "I promised you I'd tell you about my past."

"It's up to you." She moved forward. "But I'll listen if you're ready to talk."

He wrung his hands. "I told you I had a prior relationship with Paula when I was in my teens, but I'm no longer interested in pursuing it and haven't been for a long time."

"I remember." She didn't know when she'd seen Jess so nervous. How difficult could the situation be? Did she truly want to know?

"The reason I haven't said anything more about my past is because the issue I'm concerned with isn't legally confirmed as definite."

Legal issue? She tipped her head to the side. "I don't understand."

He closed his eyes and took in a deep breath. "Today after you left, I found out Paula's father recently passed away. He was wealthy, powerful and the main reason I've had no luck in reaching the family, since it's the way he wanted things. He had total control. I know how absurd it sounds, but it's the truth."

She wanted to ask why he cared so much if he and Paula were no longer involved after all these years, but held back and tapped her foot on the floor, hoping to calm her own nerves. "Go on."

Jess dragged his hand through his hair. He cleared his throat. "Paula had a baby girl and I've thought for years she was mine. Of course, Mr. Jules fired me after he realized Paula was pregnant. I understood. Yet I wanted to take responsibility, but there was no way I could do it. Mr. Jules kept Paula out of reach. Any phone calls or letters I sent remained unanswered. It was as if she'd disappeared off the earth. Now, the little girl would be over seven years old."

Lei's mouth dropped open. Her dinner threatened her throat. She didn't see this coming. "Oh, Jess. What will you do now since Paula's father is gone?"

"I'll see if I can find her and unearth the truth about everything. Paula may be more open to me now, if I can locate her. She might even be married by this time with a different last name. Who knows? This is only a beginning after such a long time."

Her knee bounced up and down under the table. "And if you do connect with Paula and the little girl, then what?"

"We'll have DNA testing if Paula agrees to it. If I'm legally identified as the father I'll offer to be in her life as much as possible, if she and Paula accept me. And I'll take responsibility as a father as best as I can, despite coming into this late. I don't have all the answers, but it's my hope." He opened the top button of his shirt and drew in a breath.

She leaned forward. "This could change your entire life. Jess, I take it you'll be leaving Hawaii for the mainland when it all happens."

"If it happens. But not for good." He rubbed his hands over his pant legs. "I was mindful this could happen before I made the move to Hawaii. Visits with her here, there, or by phone would be great. You're aware I'm planning to go to Oahu in time. I'll also have more capital with a better job to offset travel costs and help financially as a father."

Her eyes widened, but her voice remained soft and halting. This was big, huge. "I can tell you I understand the feelings of a child not having a parent. She is your first priority. And I truly hope you get the matter settled for all of your sakes. I can't imagine what you've gone through over the years."

Jess gazed upward and pressed a hand over his heart. "Thank you. I appreciate it. I know it's a big deal."

Body rigid, she fixed her stare on him. "Once you see her, can you honestly say you won't want to move back to the mainland? You say you won't, but how can you be sure? I don't think it's possible until this is settled and you see her. Only then will you decide how you want to live the rest of your life in relation to Paula and this child. I understand, but I do wish you had mentioned the possibility earlier."

"I've had years to contemplate this, and I'm fine with the plans I've made for my future." Jess stood. "I do apologize for not telling you sooner, but up until this morning after you left, there wasn't much reason to think this could happen. I've searched for years and came up with nothing." He tilted his head and squinted. "But how would it have made a difference for you if I'd said something sooner? I need to know."

She cared for him more than she'd admitted to herself. "I would've known about the possibility and could have kept it in mind as to how our relationship may or may not have evolved. There's a possibility for you living or spending a lot of time on the mainland, especially with such a distance between you and the little girl, for you to consider as a father."

"You said you would've kept the possibility in mind. Does it mean my having a child would have affected how you felt towards me?"

She gasped. Her voice rose. "Of course, not. I love all children and like to help them any way I can."

His pitch increased. "What then? I don't understand."

Lei's chin trembled. "A child changes everything for you Jess, even the best of intended plans. I don't want to get my heart set on something and not have it work out the way you hope it does. I need to consider stability in my life, not having had much of it."

Jess stepped closer to her, his voice deafening. "You think I'm not stable if I have a child?"

With elbows on the table, Lei clenched both fists, hoping to stop the trembling. "No, Jess. Not you." She glanced up at him, searching his eyes. "Me. I wouldn't have gotten so involved if I thought you might have to go back to the mainland. I think a child is an excellent reason to do so. Maybe I think so more than you do at the moment. But for me, it's hard to lose the people close to me."

He placed his palms against the table. "You're getting way ahead of the situation. This is why I didn't want to say anything until I was sure, and I'm a long way from any certainty yet. I wasn't trying to be dishonest. I care about you and want you in my life. Don't you believe me?"

Heaving out a breath, she quivered inside. "It isn't about believing you in this moment. It's about the direction of your life with a child. The rest of our feelings don't matter right now."

Jess came around the side of the table and caressed her shoulder. "I think they do."

Lei flinched at his touch. Time to protect herself again, like during her childhood without her parents. She stood and stumbled back a step. "Thanks for your honesty. I do appreciate it and know it couldn't have been easy to tell me. Honestly, I am glad for you to finally have a better opportunity to pursue this." Her thoughts spun and time stopped. "I-I should go home."

He hugged her, his voice soft. "Lei, I'm so sorry. I do love you and never meant to upset you."

"I know you didn't and don't be sorry. When I asked for the truth, you complied." She wanted to tell him she loved him too, but couldn't. It didn't matter right now. Her eyes watered. "You have a big responsibility to fill. Please don't make promises you might not be able to keep in the future, even if they're well-meaning at this moment."

"I'll do anything to gain your trust. Please don't leave and give up on us."

"I do trust you, Jess. You were honest with me about this child. But it's not so much about our relationship or my trusting you, it's about your possibility of having a child. And I'm not going anywhere. This is my homeland. My life is here. I don't need anything at the moment, but your child does. I'm not unhappy about it, but saying she comes first before either of us." Lei pulled away and dashed out the kitchen door, across the lawn, through the hibiscus bushes and into the plantation house. With the door closed behind her, she took a deep breath and let the tears flow.

When had she let herself fall in love with Jess? And right on the heels of dealing with Eric. Foolish girl.

Now, how to calm herself. Lei flipped on the kitchen light and spread out on the living room sofa. A good night's sleep would help her figure things out and let go of the emotion experienced tonight. Sleep. Yeah, right.

At the sewing machine, she finished the children's cartoon-like *menehune* outfits. The small, mythical beings taunted her, showing their high-spirited smiles.

Lei couldn't stay busy enough to keep her mind calm right now. Maybe she'd call Malia before it got much later and check on her and Jenny. Tomorrow she'd consider volunteering time helping kids with their reading at King Kamehameha III elementary, since the new business had improved and she'd gained more capital. And pursue more information about her father, too. Yes, this should all help distract her from Jess for a while.

She drew in a deep breath. The next steps in her life together with Jess depended on how his search would turn out and what he decided to do.

*

Late the next afternoon at home, Lei searched the Internet for information about her father. Glad she remembered the town he'd come from in Ohio, she searched for him in the area.

His name surfaced. An obituary. She closed her eyes a moment, breaths shallow. It stung, but it shouldn't have. In a way, she'd long ago mourned him after he'd left them. But as a drug addict, his demise shouldn't surprise her at all. Their father expired at a place called County Rehabilitation Center. Had he been trying to rehabilitate right at the end? She gazed at the laptop again. He'd passed away several years later after he'd left Maui, around the time her mother had died. Tears stung her eyes. She read through the details of the article and reread the line which surprised her the most.

Mr. Mark Hudson is survived by a daughter, Catherine Hudson, of Toledo, Ohio.

Her father had another child, a half-sister to her, Malia and Kimo. Her mind in a flurry and light-headed, she couldn't think and closed the laptop. She'd put it in the back of her mind for now, and needed to process the information before alerting anyone.

She reclined on the couch, her eyes heavy, but she'd promised to deliver Mrs. Chen's order before dinner. She entered the bedroom and grabbed the tablecloth and placemats for the woman's daughter.

The screen door clattered from a heavy knock.

Lei glanced out of the bedroom doorway. "Mrs. Chen. I was about to come over with your order." She unlocked the screen door and held it open for her friend.

As usual, the older woman handed her a basket. "I make 'em fresh today. *Malasadas.*"

A whiff of the deep fried, donut-like pastries made her salivate. "Thank you. I love them. Please have a seat. I'll get your items."

She returned with the colorful yellow and green pineapple patterned material. "I hope your daughter likes them."

Mrs. Chen unfolded the tablecloth and surveyed the matching placemats. "Oh, lovely. If my Rosie don't like 'em, I keep 'em." A palm came over her mouth and she giggled. "How much I owe you?"

"Nothing. Please accept it for my appreciation of all you've done for me. I'm doing well at work, and I want to give back."

"Mahalo. My daughter comes this weekend. How is your *'ohana?*"

"The family's doing as well as can be expected. My tutu finds it hard to get around but does all right. My brother is settled down and looking for work, but my sister is upset yet about her friend in the hospital from the car accident."

She squinted. "Oh, yeah. Too bad. What a horrible thing someone did to them."

"Yes." She grabbed a pitcher from the fridge. "Will you have some of my green, iced tea?"

"Sure. And when you come back and sit with me, I want to hear about you."

Her brows scrunched together as she poured the tea. "What do you mean? I've told you my news." She returned to the chair.

Mrs. Chen took the glass from her and pointed an index finger at Lei. "I said you."

"I'm fine. I like living here and I'm planning to volunteer helping kids at the school now, too." She took a sip of the cold, green tea.

"Good. Anything else?" The woman tipped her head.

Would Jess have told Mrs. Chen about them and his possible child so soon? "No, I don't think so."

"Would Jess agree? He looked worried, so I asked what bothered him. Part of it is about his child. But there's more. I just know."

Lei squeezed her eyes shut a moment and sighed. "Yes. We need to take it easy until he settles his life and decides how he wants to proceed. The little girl lives on the mainland. If he finds the child, I won't stand in his way."

Mrs. Chen leaned forward. "But he loves you. Having a child doesn't change his feelings for you."

"I understand it doesn't change how he feels about me." She flipped her hair behind her shoulders. "And I care for him, too. But a child comes first."

"I know you care for him. I see the two of you and you have something special. Don't throw it away. Do you want to go through life with no one close to love?"

"But he may want to go back to the mainland with his child for good. I understand it, yet I don't want to lose him and get hurt."

"What's the worst thing that could happen if you leave here? Who says you have to lose him?" Mrs. Chen sat back in the chair and folded her arms across her chest.

Her voice rose. "Maui is a stable force in my life. It's what I know. What little family I have left lives here. When all else fails or others leave my life, I can count on my homeland to remain for me, and God, of course."

"Jess understands your wishes are important, too. But you have to decide what's most important. For now, your work and home matter most. I get it. But wait and see." She wagged an index finger toward her chest. "For me, I raised my two kids, my husband's boy and one by *hanai*, who didn't have any 'ohana to care for him. Love them all. A blessing for all of us."

"Wow. I didn't know you'd adopted a child who had no family. How fortunate all of your kids were to have you." Mrs. Chen was even more loving and special than Lei realized.

Mrs. Chen shoved the glass away. "Life happens in unusual ways sometimes. You work it out. I know you like kids. Maybe you can help this girl who was raised without her father. Who knows?"

She placed her hand over her throat. "Me?"

"Sure. You help others." Mrs. Chen's shoulders curled over her chest, arms crossed in front of her. "I wish I could have one more day with Mr. Chen anywhere in the world in any situation. One more day."

"I wish you could, too." Her chin quivered. "What a special love you two had. It must be so difficult for you without him." She rose and hugged Mrs. Chen. "But you're a special lady and I'm so glad you came into my life. You've given me something to think about. I have to consider my feelings for Jess regardless of the circumstances. Thank you so much."

Mrs. Chen rose, patted Lei's shoulder, picked up the tablecloth and placemats and held them in front of her. "And mahalo, thank you again for these." The older woman headed out the door.

Lei hooked the screen latch and closed the inside door. Could she handle the vulnerability which came with love? And the strength to deal with whatever happened next while Jess moved forward to find his daughter? If not, their relationship would come to an end. She'd have to make a choice in time.

In the bedroom, she turned on the lamp at the bedside table. She pulled the list of Scripture passages Pastor Kane had given her from inside the Bible and read a verse from Hebrews 10:9. *"Behold, I have come to do your will, O God."* Would she ever realize what her destiny entailed, or where she truly belonged in this life?

Sitting on the bed, Lei placed the Scripture passages back in the Bible and would hope and pray for answers in time.

The phone buzzed. Malia.

"I'm afraid I have some dreadful news."

A flush of heat rushed into her throat and she jerked back. "What's happened?"

"Tutu fell, hit her head and it's serious." Malia's voice shook. "I'm at the hospital. She might not make it."

She gasped. With eyes squeezed shut, her breath hitched. "I'll—I'll come right now."

Tears streaming down her cheeks, she grabbed her purse. Her precious Tutu.

CHAPTER ELEVEN

Forty-five minutes later, Lei stormed through the hospital emergency department doors. Malia sat in the corner, head in her hands next to Dirk.

She rushed to Malia's side. "Have you heard anymore?"

"Only a moment ago. Tutu's brain wave activity isn't normal from all the trauma and damage done. She isn't able to respond at all." Malia continued to choke out the words. "She lost blood, has broken bones and internal injuries. Despite what they've done for her, there isn't any hope. There's nothing more they can do to help our grandmother."

Dizzy, she shook, grabbed Malia's hand and sat beside her. "No. How can this be?"

With a hand on each of their shoulders, Dirk stood in front of her and Malia. "They said we could see Tutu soon and to be prepared. We haven't been able to reach Kimo. He's not answering."

Dirk's voice echoed somewhere in the background. Lei stared at her palms resting on her lap, as if they held the answers she wanted to hear.

A young nurse in blue scrubs entered the waiting area and signaled them to follow her. Dirk walked behind the nurse, followed by Malia and Lei. There in the small, dim-lit room lay Tutu on a hospital bed with an oxygen mask, her face as gray as her hair. *How could this happen?*

Malia sobbed, and Dirk moved closer to comfort her.

A heavy feeling in Lei's stomach lingered, but she had to touch Tutu. Her grandmother's cold hand lay heavy against her own, as if life had slipped from it. Tears fell.

With shoulders slumped, Lei lowered her head toward Tutu. Her chin trembled as she spoke. "You are and have been a bright presence in my life. No one can ever change the special bond we had together. I love you so much, Tutu, forever. Rest in God's embrace." She stared at the nurse. "I'd like for the chaplain to come, please."

The nurse nodded and left the room.

All three of them stood by Tutu's side in the quiet of the room. Lei continued to hold Tutu's hand and also held Malia's hand.

Hot tears drifted down her cheeks. *Lord, thy will be done. May Tutu rest in Your peace and love.*

Numb, she stood motionless while time halted.

The repetitive beep from a machine turned into a continuous hum. The nurse entered the room, silenced the monitor and removed Tutu's oxygen mask. "I'm so sorry for your loss. The chaplain is on his way."

Breathless, Lei took a step back. A sudden coldness filled her core. The beautiful matriarch who'd loved them and did her best to hold their scattered 'ohana together left them and this world.

WHERE SHE BELONGS

*

The next morning, Lei awakened at Malia's apartment in Jenny's bedroom and remembered immediately Tutu had passed away. Should she call Jess? She wanted to, but what did she expect him to do after depending on him as much as she had? Body aching, stiff and tense from the sleepless night, she stood next to the bed and put on a robe Malia had lent her.

Shuffling into the kitchen, she witnessed poor Malia standing there red-eyed and embraced her.

Malia's tears fell again, and she stuttered. "I-I'm having trouble believing Tutu's gone."

"Me, too. It happened so fast. I can't wrap my head around it yet. It's like a bad, recurring nightmare."

Lei poured some coffee and sat at the small counter. The steam and smell helped wake her a little. "Today we'll have to clear Tutu's home at the assisted living facility, get the will and plan a funeral." With a down-turned mouth, her voice lacked strength. "Just what one wants to tackle after losing a loved one."

"For sure." Malia grasped her coffee mug in both hands, as if it would fall. "Dirk called me this morning. Kimo and Elle got in late last night. He told them about Tutu and has also set up an appointment with the attorney later this morning at eleven o'clock."

A gulp of the potent Kona brew moistened her dry throat. "Good. I'm glad he caught up with Kimo and also made the appointment, since he handles most of Tutu's financial affairs. I'll call the hotel to notify them I won't be in to work today. This morning we'll retrieve Tutu's copy of the will from the safe deposit box at the bank first. After the meeting at the attorney's office, we'll clear out her belongings this afternoon and set up the memorial service. Then I'll head back home." Tense fingers laced around the white ceramic mug. "There's a pastor in Lahaina I'd like to perform the service, if it's okay with you."

"Fine with me." Malia rinsed out the coffee mug. "Let me know when you're ready to leave."

After downing a muffin, she dressed and they headed for the bank. Inside the safe deposit room, Lei pulled out the keyring and unlocked Tutu's box. "Here's the will." The paper crinkled as she lifted it from the lock box and unfolded it.

They read it and stared at each other.

Malia's eyes widened. "Did you know you were the executor, Lei?"

She touched her throat and gasped. "No, I didn't. I thought it would be Dirk."

"Me, too."

Heat flushed across Lei's cheeks. "Surprising. He's not even mentioned to receive anything in this will. The remainder of the estate is split amongst the three of us siblings."

Malia touched fingers to her lips. "It's unexpected, don't you think?"

"Yeah. Do you suppose he's aware of it?"

Lei closed the lock box and stashed the copy of the will in her purse. "We'll find out soon enough with the reading of the will at the attorney's office."

They drove through downtown Kahului to the attorney's building. Inside, the receptionist directed them into the lawyer's office.

Dirk nodded when they came into the room. Kimo sat at Dirk's right side. He stood, opened his arms and hugged Lei and Malia.

Mr. Hopkins, a stout, bald middle-aged man entered the room and extended his hand to each of them. With a jerky motion, Lei shook his hand. She sat next to Malia, who sat next to Dirk.

After greeting everyone, the attorney sat at his desk. "I'm Rich Hopkins. I'd like to start with some preliminary information first."

She bit her lip and sat rigid in the chair while Mr. Hopkins explained the legalities and probate.

"Before I continue on, you all have my sincere sympathy." He glanced at the will. "This will was updated not long ago and is in proper order. Leilani Hudson is designated as the executor."

A quick sideways glance toward Dirk showed him motionless and staring straight ahead, but he blinked several times.

Palms sweaty, Lei shook them out. Total quietness in the room. Only the ruffling of the paper as the attorney turned the page.

Mr. Hopkins cleared his throat. "The remainder of the estate will be equally divided between Leilani Hudson, Malia Hudson and Kimo Hudson. The maʻkua collection goes to the owner of the plantation house." He glanced back and forth at all of them.

Lei raised a hand. "I own the plantation house."

The man tipped his head to the side. "Do you have these fishhooks, Miss Hudson?"

"No, I don't. We can't seem to find them." She rubbed her palms together. A sideways glance showed Kimo's shoulders curled forward, his chin dipped low near his chest.

"Well if you do find them, they're legally yours. I'll contact you during and of course, after the probate period. Let me know if there are any questions or concerns in the meantime. Thank you all for coming in today and again, I give you my heartfelt condolences."

With arms crossed, Dirk continued to stare ahead for a moment. He stepped across the aisle and over to Mr. Hopkins.

Thinking it best to leave him alone, she entered the reception area, followed by Malia.

"Wait a moment, won't you, please?" Dirk rushed up to them.

Lei halted in mid stride and her pulse rose. "Of course."

Kimo stepped near her. "Did you know who would receive the maʻkua?"

With hands clasped, her eye twitched. "No. I didn't know until today."

He glanced downward. "I'm sorry about them and well, everything. They're rightfully yours, wherever they are."

Lei faced Dirk. "Let me say I'm sorry, Dirk. We didn't know about the will's contents before this morning." He hadn't questioned the will, but somehow Lei hoped an apology might be worth something.

"I'm not concerned with the subject matter listed in the will, but I would've thought your grandmother should have alerted you about the executorship." Dirk stared at her. "I've handled several and it's a big responsibility, especially if you're not used to dealing with them."

Lei fidgeted with her hands. "Tutu never told us too much regarding her personal or financial transactions. I guess she wanted to keep our family time separate from business." She drew in a breath. "If you remember, none of us knew about the inheritance we received from Tutu according to your great uncle's wishes not so long ago either."

"I did. I suppose it's why I thought she'd alert you about the will." Dirk fidgeted with his tie.

"Oh. I didn't realize you were aware of those gifts." Not knowing what else to say, Lei glanced downward a moment.

"I've helped her for a long time with the business interests except for this will, of course. Otherwise, I could've made you aware of it if I'd known, so you would've had warning." Dirk's brows rose. "It's an added responsibility along with grief, the funeral and everything else needing to be done."

Malia faced Dirk. "We all appreciate the great help you've given her."

"Dirk." Lei paused. "Besides the shock of Tutu's death, the will is a surprise to all of us. I don't know what to say to you at this point. I don't know how much capital will remain in the estate after probate, but we do feel bad you weren't included. There's not much we can do about it right now."

Kimo pulled his navy T-shirt down near his hips and glanced upward at Dirk.

Dirk's face reddened, and a sheen of sweat beaded on his forehead. The man turned toward Lei. "Oh, I didn't expect any money. I'm only surprised she didn't say something to you. If you want, I can help you with any of the duties since I'm used to dealing with finances, especially for your grandmother. Sorry, I didn't mean to keep you. My apologies. And please accept my sympathy for the loss of your grandmother, ladies."

"How kind of you, Dirk. I definitely appreciate it. Thank you so much." Lei breathed easier, with Dirk not harboring resentment over not receiving any compensation.

After Dirk and Kimo left the office reception area, Lei faced her sister. "Dirk's surprise at Tutu's will is understandable. We were shocked, too. But I feel a little better now after talking with him."

"He's so used to helping and being involved. I forgot to tell you he was with Tutu when she fell. I'm so glad she wasn't alone when it happened. He called the nurse into the room to help and they contacted the emergency department right away. It's some consolation knowing everything was done for Tutu as soon as possible."

"Yeah, it's good to know. But I have so many mixed feelings right now. I'd offer to let Dirk help with the executor duties, but then I might feel I'm taking advantage of him, too. I have to let this all sink in for a while." Lei rubbed tired eyes. "Let's get Tutu's belongings collected now. I need to return home and speak with the pastor."

"Have you talked to Jess yet?"

Jess. How she wished she could lean on him now, but it was too much to ask of him. They'd left each other at odds. "No. I'll tell him in time."

Malia tipped her head. "Is there a problem with you two?"

"No, Malia. He has issues going on in his life, too. It isn't fair to dump this on him right now. Besides, I have an executorship to figure out now. We have to stay focused on dealing with Tutu's death, the funeral plans, and the will on top of everything else."

Lei couldn't deal with her feelings regarding Jess now, but she did swear Malia had radar at times.

After processing everything, Lei would consider approaching him.

CHAPTER TWELVE

Two days after Tutu's memorial service, Lei prepared for the distribution of Tutu's ashes at sea. Sun reflected off the red and yellow outrigger canoe at Kahului. A warm, breeze caressed Lei's face while the vessel shifted back and forth. Tutu loved the sea breeze and ocean. And thankfully, Jess had become Lei's rock.

With Malia seated across from Lei, Jess and Pastor Kane shoved them off into the water, hopped in and paddled away from the shore. Kimo, Elle and Dirk's canoe pressed on ahead of them. The waves rocked the outrigger as they paddled farther out to sea. Such a beautiful, sunny day, one Tutu would've enjoyed.

With both canoes side by side, Pastor Kane's final prayer brought tears to her eyes. Jess tightened his grip around her shoulder the exact moment she needed extra support. What would she have done without him during this time?

After a blessing in Hawaiian, Pastor Kane looked at each of them. "We fulfill your grandmother's last wishes by returning her ashes to the ocean she loved so much. Her remains leave us, but her spirit is everlasting." He took the urn and scattered the ashes alongside the canoe into the ocean.

Tears slid down Lei's face again as she removed the purple, orchid lei she wore and tossed it into the Pacific. Everyone else followed suit and soon a beautiful group of flower leis bobbed in the waves.

The men grabbed their paddles for their return journey while a pod of dolphins frolicked in front of them for a moment.

Malia caught Lei's gaze. "Tutu is free now, like the dolphins. No more canes or walkers needed and no more pain."

"Yes. We can be thankful she's at peace and not suffering." She stared out at the ocean until she could no longer see the leis.

At shore, Jess helped Lei and Malia disembark from the canoe. The others in the second canoe followed.

Lei put a hand above her eyes to shade them from the piercing sun. She faced Pastor Kane. "Mahalo for a wonderful service. You made it so special for us."

"You're most welcome. Remember, anytime you want to talk, I'm here." Pastor placed his hand on her shoulder. "God's blessings on all of you. Aloha."

Lei returned a wave from Elle and Kimo.

"Let me know if there's anything I can do." Dirk stepped closer to her and shook her hand.

"I will. Thank you, Dirk." Lei headed toward Jess's car with her sister at her side. "Ready to leave, Malia?"

Her voice softened. "I guess we have to be."

Jess dropped Malia off at her apartment, and they continued through the central valley with the West Maui Mountains to their right and Haleakalā Crater to their left, typically shrouded in clouds more often than not. Stability. Yes, Lei could count on the beauty of her island homeland for comfort, as well as the Lord.

Jess glanced at her and wrinkled his brow. "Are you doing okay?"

"Yeah, but I feel like I have a hole in my heart. Is it wrong to wish Tutu would've been okay? Or somehow the fall shouldn't have happened?"

"No, of course, it's not wrong. It's understandable and will take you a while to process your grandmother's passing, especially since it was so sudden and unexpected. I'm here for you." He patted her shoulder.

But was he? For how long? "I appreciate all you've done, but I realize you have a life, too."

"Don't worry about me. I'm doing fine." He clutched the wheel tighter with both hands. "I meant to ask if you'd heard any more about the investigation regarding Malia's car and Jenny's state of health."

Maybe he didn't want to talk about his life. "Jenny is doing the same. It's tough on her parents and Malia. As for the investigation, they've followed the leads and haven't found anything yet." Her voice rose. "Nothing. Not one thing."

"I'm so sorry. Give it time and don't give up on them. Maybe if the person commits another crime and is apprehended, which often happens, justice will take place. Something should turn up eventually. There has to be someone on this island who knows what happened."

"I would think so." She blew out a breath.

"How about the Internet search you planned to do?" Jess glanced at her. "Did you have a chance to get at it before your tutu passed on?"

"As a matter of fact, I did."

"And did you have any luck?"

"Yes. My father's dead, not surprisingly. It happened around the same time as my mom's passing."

He squeezed her forearm. "I'm sorry. I shouldn't have asked you today."

"Don't be. I knew in my heart years ago he wouldn't survive long. He died in a rehab facility. And he had another child."

"Wow." His brows rose. "It must have come as quite a surprise."

"Definitely. I've told Malia and Kimo, and I'll give it a rest for now. But it's good I'm aware of the circumstances and facts."

"Yeah, it's the main thing. I hope it helps you in time." Jess rounded the curve and tiny Molokini Crater came into view, peeking out above the ocean.

In silence, with only the hum of car tires until they passed through the tunnel heading toward Lahaina, she couldn't think of anything more to say. Tired, she leaned back into the headrest, her eyes heavy as they headed home.

Attentive as ever, Jess glanced at her. "You're tired."

"Yeah. I don't want to talk about the funeral or my family anymore. Why don't you tell me how your search is going and get my mind off Tutu for a while?"

"It's coming along okay." He bit his lip.

What did he mean? A vague response often meant someone wanted to hide information or wasn't willing to share. She tapped her fingers on her thigh. "I don't understand. If you don't want to talk about it, you don't have to tell me. It's fine."

"It isn't that I don't want to disclose my findings." He paused. "Today was your grandmother's funeral. I didn't think it appropriate to discuss my personal stuff."

"Okay." After taking the bypass around Lahaina, traffic quieted on Front Street as they passed by the houses, so close to home. Too late to discuss anything more with Jess. He was right. Maybe she didn't want to know any more information today.

After turning into his driveway, the dust settled. She grabbed her purse and the door handle.

Jess put his hand on her shoulder. "Will you be all right alone at your house?"

"Of course." She tilted her head. "I've been alone many times on difficult days."

He gazed into her eyes. "Look." His speech became rapid and jerky. "I definitely didn't want to give the impression I'm keeping something from you or I'm making an excuse not to share the search since the funeral took place today."

"It's been a long day." She squeezed the back of her neck. "I told you it was fine."

"No." His tone increased. "I don't want to leave you wondering about the Internet search, so I'll answer the question now."

She stared at him, unsure of what he meant. "Whatever you want to do, Jess."

"I received an email from Eva Rose's mother, Paula today, right before we left for the funeral."

Her mouth gaped open. "Oh, wow. And you had to keep it in all day. I'm so sorry it got stifled with our sad day and the funeral." She moved closer to him. "I apologize. You're right. I'm obviously not in the best frame of mind today. But I do hope you're pleased with the information you received."

"Yes, definitely. And Paula even sent me some recent photos of Eva Rose."

"It sounds like Paula welcomes you as Eva Rose's father, which is great. I'm so happy for you, Jess. I truly am."

"I didn't have a chance to answer Paula or ask questions so I don't know too much." His knuckles grazed her cheek. "I'll give you a call tomorrow after I've had a chance to connect with her."

She squeezed his forearm. "Okay. Thanks for coming today. I don't know what I would've done without you. It meant a lot. More than you know."

He gave her a peck on the cheek. "I'm glad I could be there for you."

"Me, too." She opened the car door and managed a grin. She meandered across the yard, through the bushes and into the house. Dropping her purse on the end table, she collapsed on the couch.

With the reality of Tutu's death sinking in after the scattering of ashes, Jess on the other hand, pursued Eva Rose as a newcomer into his life. Lei cared about Jess and hoped for the best for him and Eva Rose despite the fact it left their relationship at a crossroads.

Life went on, but one didn't necessarily know what the future might hold or the effect of losing the people one loved, as time passed. Lei more than understood the concept and would miss Tutu forever, but would she also end up losing Jess? She couldn't shake the feeling no matter how hard she tried.

*

After changing out of his casual aloha attire and into a T-shirt and blue jean shorts, Jess sat at the kitchen table, opened the laptop and grabbed the photos of Eva Rose he'd printed off in the morning before attending the scattering of ashes. He'd check on Lei later.

He ran his thumb over the close-up photo, studying Eva Rose's every feature. She resembled Paula, yet Eva Rose's hair and eye color mirrored his own. Glancing at the full-body portrait of her, Eva Rose looked tall in comparison to the chair next to her, or so he thought. Could she be lanky like he'd been? Regardless, she was a beautiful, child. He wanted to know everything about her.

Jess placed the pictures aside. He would shop for frames soon to grace the walls with photos of his precious child. He pulled the laptop closer and reread the last few paragraphs of the email.

Sorry it's been so long since we've communicated, but you know the reason why. If I tried to leave or reach out to you, my father promised to make it difficult for you. I knew him well, so I didn't doubt his determination and powerful capabilities. Yet he was my father and cared for Eva Rose and me. Young as I was, I didn't have much choice at the time but to remain under his thumb. There were other issues I won't go into which led me to stay, but they don't matter now. Eva Rose's welfare came first then and always will. Why waste time and energy on a past we can't change?

Due to my father's hand, you weren't designated as Eva Rose's father on her birth certificate. We can take measures to formally verify and certify you as her father, if you like.

I'll gladly answer any questions you have. In the meantime,
I thought you'd enjoy these photos of Eva Rose.
   Paula

Jess's shoulders dropped and a weight lifted from him. He tapped his fingers on the table, definitely wanting the legalities of his child certified in writing and never challenged in any way by anyone again.

Where to begin? Paula welcomed his questions. He wanted to speak his true mind and wishes regarding Eva Rose, but should he proceed at a slow pace? He didn't want to risk upsetting Eva Rose's life and ruining their chances of a relationship with the enormous zeal he harbored. But it wouldn't hurt to call his boss today and see if there was an opportunity for him to squeeze in a trip to the mainland, in case.

Jess shoved his chair back from the table and strode across the vinyl floor to the kitchen window. He planted his hands on the windowsill and stared out toward Lei's house. Had she been correct when she said he couldn't predict how he'd feel once he forged a relationship with his daughter? Evidently, Lei had a better handle on Jess's feelings than he did himself. Look how his attitude changed in one day.

Eyes closed, he rubbed the middle of his forehead. For years he'd searched for the opportunity to connect with his child. Now, given the opportunity, he didn't know how to handle it and lost control of his emotions when he thought he never would. He wanted to see his child, and the sooner the better. Period.

Jess returned to the table. Fretting over what to say to Paula didn't help. He'd give her his phone number so they could discuss the situation more easily and let her know he'd had his DNA analysis performed previously. In his email, he'd ask if he could meet Eva Rose and would pray for a positive response.

*

The next morning, Jess awoke early. Unable to wait any longer before checking his email, he threw on a T-shirt and shorts and headed for the kitchen. He booted up the laptop and hoped Paula had sent a reply back to him.

Jess shook out his sweaty palms as he stared at the screen. He clicked the mouse to open his email account and scanned new mail.

Yes. A reply from Paula. His pulse throbbed in his ears as he read it.

Jess,

You can meet with Eva Rose. I have spoken with her about you and I've told her what I feel she can understand about us as her parents. We will have to take it slow and see how she does. I'll have Eva Rose's DNA analysis performed. And when it's completed, I'll start any other paternity testing necessary and any legal action claiming you as her biological father. I'll let you know if you need bloodwork taken in addition to the DNA, too. Hopefully, everything will be completed and in order, and you will only need to sign the legal forms whenever you arrive.

Here are some interests Eva Rose enjoys, so you can more easily visit with her when you meet her. She loves dancing lessons, is a good student and likes reading. Anything to do with horses creates an easy conversation with her, too. Attached are a few more photographs for you.

I'll call you later on today, when it's early morning in your time zone.

Paula

Energy surging through his body, Jess thrust a fist into the air. He downloaded the photos, hit the print button and hurried over to the printer as it hummed, clicked and dropped the photos into the tray. He stared at each one. His child smiling and posing in a blue, dance costume. The other showing Eva Rose sitting on a horse in a riding outfit.

He pressed both pictures to his chest, blinked back tears and choked up for a moment.

After placing the new photos with the others on the table, Jess grabbed some mixed fruit from the fridge and brewed some coffee. He finished his few personal care chores in readiness for Paula's call.

Back at the table, he finished the last chunk of pineapple and sipped at his coffee. He savored the flavor of strong brew, but for once didn't need the jolt of caffeine one expected from morning coffee. The prospect of meeting his child more than did the trick.

Tapping his foot against the floor, he checked the time and glanced at his phone on the table. What would it be like to hear Paula's voice again after so many years? What would he say? He'd had years to rehearse such a conversation, but the thoughts eluded him now.

And what about Lei? Was she sitting by the phone waiting for him to call? He hoped not. Jess glanced out the window in the direction of her house. She had dealt with so much. He appreciated her genuine happiness for him, but how did she feel inside?

The phone rang and he jolted from his chair. He recognized the area code. Paula.

He cleared his throat. "Hello."

"Jess, how are you?"

He'd have known her voice anywhere. "I'm great. And you and Eva Rose?"

"We're doing well."

His turn to speak. Now what to say? "I-uh. I've checked with my boss at work. My job is temporary, so I can either wait until it ends before I come to the mainland or he's willing to give me some time off soon which I can make up later. What works for you?"

"I'm free. You set the date and let me know. Eva Rose has school, so over a weekend would be a good start. She can also miss a day or two and I could get assignments ahead of time if necessary. We can work on the details of completing the forms for you becoming Eva Rose's legal father during the weekdays, too."

Warmth radiated throughout his body as blood surged through his veins. "Wonderful. How about if I plan to arrive on a Friday or Saturday and take it from there? I'll get back to you with a date as soon as possible."

"Great. We'll be waiting to hear from you."

We. His daughter and Paula. Could this be real? "Paula, what would you suggest I say or how should I approach Eva Rose?"

"She's a strong, determined little girl, a lot like you. Be yourself with her and you'll be fine."

Like him. His voice shook. "Thank you, Paula, for everything."

Today he'd schedule the time off with his boss and then make plane and hotel reservations.

A glance at his watch revealed he had time to give Lei a call before they both left for work. He punched in the number and tapped his foot on the floor. The phone rang three times.

"Hello, Jess."

"Morning. If you have a minute, would you stop by? Come right in."

"Okay. I'm on the way."

He rubbed his palms together, walked to the counter and poured a cup of coffee for her.

The screen door creaked open.

Her beautiful dark hair flowed over her shoulders and tumbled onto the red and white mu'umu'u she wore. He set the coffee cup on the table. "Just in time for some Kona brew."

"Thanks. I won't turn down a cup of coffee." She sat at the table.

Jess sat across from her and took a sip from his coffee. "I've got so much to tell you. I talked with Eva Rose's mother. She acknowledges me as Eva Rose's father, and I feel the same."

"Sounds like a good start."

His tone increased. "Yes, but it gets better. They'll perform DNA testing which verifies Eva Rose's biological connection to me and I'll also be designated as the father on the birth certificate." He leaned forward. "But the best news is I've been invited to meet my daughter."

Her hand squeezed his forearm. "Oh, Jess. I'm sure it's a dream come true for you."

"I can't believe it's a reality yet." He ran his thumb back and forth over the side of the cup.

Lei stared at the photos of Eva Rose. "So this is your daughter. She's beautiful. I can see where she resembles you."

His heart drummed in his chest. "You think so?"

"Yes, I do."

His chest thrusted outward. "Thank you."

She slid her chair closer to the table. "What does all this change mean for you now?"

"I'll make a trip to the mainland soon and stay at a hotel for up to a week. I'll set it up today with my boss."

Lei tipped her head to the side. "And after the visit?"

"While I'm there, paternity testing and DNA will have been completed, so I'll sign legal documents Paula is having prepared for me as Eva Rose's father. It's a matter of getting the technical and legal stuff out of the way." But how would he feel when he saw Paula and his child? Lei showed honest compassion for him, but did her interest slip in regard to their relationship now?

"Will you have custody?" She sipped the coffee.

"No custody discussions at this point. Right now, I want the legal designation as her father and to take any responsibility for however it best suits Eva Rose. This is a major change for her, more than the rest of us put together."

"Especially for her." She gazed downward. "Will you return here and stay on in Hawaii like you planned?"

Lei had a right to know. He exhaled. "I'll return."

"What will you do if you get offered the Oahu position with all of this happening for you?"

Jess raised his voice. "I'll deal with it if and when it happens." He hadn't even thought about the Oahu employment since finding Eva Rose.

"Thanks for filling me in and for the coffee, but it's time to get going. You'll have a wonderful time on your trip." She rose and met his gaze. "Jess, I'm so happy for you."

"I know you are. You've been fantastic about everything." Jess walked over to her and placed his arm around her shoulder. "I promise to keep in touch." He pushed his fingers through his hair. "I don't have all the answers yet and am anxious about everything. As of right now, my plans haven't changed drastically, but I do need to meet my child." Maybe he should have told Lei she'd been right about how his feelings might change, but now it would only add more stress on their relationship.

Her eyes widened. "Of course, you do. I would think less of you if you didn't. Please don't think I'm the type of person who would come between the two of you. I'd never try to keep a child from a parent. My concern is to know how things will work out for both of you and your tentative plans."

"I understand." He lowered his forehead to hers. "This is a big change for all of us."

The cell phone rang. She glanced at the caller ID and pulled back. "It's Malia. She never calls this early in the morning unless something's amiss. Again, thanks for letting me know and good luck with your plans. Bye, Jess." She sprinted out of the house and the screen door clattered behind her.

An attempt to catch up with Lei later at lunchtime might be helpful. He admitted his vagueness concerning the Oahu job and even staying on indefinitely in the islands. Yeah, he'd return, but then what?

121

Back at the table he rested his arms on it and lowered his head. Now he understood Lei's comment all the better in stating a person couldn't make long-term decisions before experiencing true feelings.

Could he leave his little girl so far away once he'd spent time with her? He hadn't even met her yet and his gut reply said it would be more than difficult.

Jess wanted to be fair concerning everyone involved, but seeing Eva Rose would have a huge impact on him, without a doubt.

CHAPTER THIRTEEN

Lei scurried from Jess's house across the lawn with the phone pressed to her ear. "Hold on a second, Malia, until I get in the house so I can hear you better. I'm outside and a neighbor is mowing the lawn."

"Okay."

Out of breath, she entered the kitchen and closed the door behind her. "All right. Go ahead."

Malia's voice flattened. "I thought I'd let you know about Jenny before you went to work."

Lei sat in the kitchen chair, squeezed her eyes shut a moment and her stomach roiled. Malia's voice gave her away. It couldn't be good news. "Oh no. Tell me, please."

"Jenny's parents are having a conference with the doctors today. I'm not sure what it all means, but I do know she hasn't improved."

"No improvement is scary. It can't be a good sign the longer she stays unconscious, can it?"

"I doubt it. I don't know for sure, but I figured you'd want to know about her situation."

With elbows on the table, her voice softened. "Yes, of course I do. Thanks so much for letting me know. Will you call me back if there's more news?"

"Yeah. If you're not available, I'll leave a message on your cell if I happen to hear anymore before the day is out."

Lei shifted in the chair, unable to get comfortable. "I'll check my phone when I can. And I can close my sale tables any time at the hotel or come and be with you now if you'd like."

"No, let's wait and see what her parents have to say."

She sat back in the chair. "Okay, if you're sure."

"I could use some good news. Anything new with you?"

Lei shouldn't mention Jess for now until his plans were underway. She paused. "Malia, since I told you and Kimo about Dad and his daughter, Catherine, I also want to let you know I have decided to follow up with her. She might not even know about us or be receptive, but she is our half-sister. What you and Kimo want to do regarding Catherine is up to you, of course. Knowing for certain Dad is gone helped put me more at peace concerning him. I didn't expect it would, but it did."

"I think it's a good thing you found out what happened to him for all of us. And as for Catherine, maybe she would like to know about the rest of Dad's family here in Hawaii. I wouldn't be at all surprised."

She rubbed the back of her neck. "Possibly. And if not, I'm okay with it. I'm learning to reach out more than I have before and take a chance on things. You're right. What can it hurt?"

"Nothing. And if she is interested, I'm in, too."

"Great. I'll keep you posted."

"Lei?"

"Yeah."

Malia paused. "You can tell Jess about the conference today if you want."

After the conversation with him minutes ago, she didn't think it a wise idea. Her voice softened. "I'll see. Maybe, if I happen to see him at the hotel."

Her sister's voice grew louder. "Are you two okay? Has something changed?"

Lei squeezed her eyes shut a moment and took in a calm breath. "We're okay." She couldn't fool Malia. "Jess found out he has a seven-year-old daughter. He'll go to the mainland to meet her soon."

Malia's heightened pitch echoed through the phone. "Are you serious? Did you know about her?"

"Jess told me it was a possibility not too long ago. He said he'd searched for years and thought the child was his but had no proof and no luck finding her."

"Whoa. How do you feel about it?"

Lei squeezed the taut muscles on the back of her neck. "I'm glad for him. It doesn't matter how I feel. The bottom line is he has a child who should come first."

"I know how much you care about Jess. This is definitely a brave, unselfish and compassionate attitude and you've handled it well. Wow. I guess we never know what will pop up any day or where life will lead us."

"Definitely not. I'll hope and pray for the best with the conference. Talk to you later, Malia."

With the merchandise in the trunk of the car, she drove to the hotel and unpacked the items on a corner table in the lobby near an arrangement of red anthuriums and torch ginger. A nice breeze came through, ruffled the tablecloth and cooled her.

Whether warm from the unpacking or from the early morning news from Jess and Malia, she couldn't say.

Lei stood behind the table, folded her hands and said a prayer for Jenny and her parents. Thoughts of Jess crowded her mind. Malia had given Lei more credit than she deserved. Her emotions did a tug of war between the insecurity with Jess's future, their relationship and wanting his child to have a father foremost, even if it meant he'd move back to the mainland.

Several visitors left the outdoor dining area and entered the lobby. Background chatter filled the air as they checked out the various products for sale. Customers kept her busy most of the morning selling the purses, placemats and tablecloths with little time to think about Jess, thank heavens.

With a quiet moment at hand, she checked the phone. No missed calls from Malia. She refilled the table with some of the stock she kept stashed under the table. A man walked toward her from the side. She turned in his direction. Jess.

He caught sight of the table and stared at the *menehune* dresses. "Looks like you've been busy today. I noticed you've replenished your items for sale."

Heat rose to her cheeks. Jess had watched her before he came to the table. "Yes, it's been busy all morning, but regardless, I do plan to leave a little early today. Can I help you with something?"

Jess pointed at the dresses. "Can you tell me which one of these might fit a child of seven?"

"Earlier I sold one to a lady in this medium size." Lei held up the pink dress with the cartoon-like characters. Jess would give his daughter one of her creations? "She said her daughter was eight years old, and average size for her age. Even if it's a little large for

Eva Rose, it's better than taking it to the mainland and having it be too small for her to wear. And if it is a little large, she'll grow into it."

"All right. I'll take one for Eva Rose." Jess grabbed the billfold from his back pocket.

The tissue paper crinkled as Lei placed the folded dress in a collapsible, cardboard box and handed it to him.

A line formed between his brows. "I know you said you'd leave early today, but do you have a few minutes?"

A glance at the lobby clock revealed how the time had passed. "Wow. I didn't realize it's already noon. I'll put my sign out and let people know I'm taking a break."

"Let's go sit outside." He pointed straight ahead.

"All right."

The trade winds gusted as they sat on a bench under a white, plumeria tree. The fallen blossoms scattered and twirled around the walkway.

What else could Jess have to tell her? She curled her fists, straightened them and waited for him to begin.

He drew in a breath. "My boss has allowed me time off to go to the mainland. I'll be able to continue to work here and make up the time I missed when I return."

She fingered her necklace. "Good news for you. When will you leave?"

"As soon as I can make the arrangements. There are some vacations to fill in for later on, so my boss said now is the best time for me to leave."

She tucked wind-blown, wisps of hair behind her ear. "Thanks for letting me know. Best wishes if I don't have a chance to speak with you before you leave."

His brows squeezed together. "What do you mean? I plan to talk with you beforehand."

Why did her nerves come unglued? Palms sweaty, she was thankful when another gust of wind passed by. "I may end up spending some time in Kahului soon. Malia has some concerns to deal with right now."

"Oh, yeah?" His voice lilted upward. "What kind of concerns?"

"Jenny's parents are in conference with the doctors today." Her voice softened. "Jenny hasn't improved. I'll spend some time with Malia, depending how the situation works. I'm waiting to hear back from her. I don't think it sounds good."

"I'm sorry. I meant to ask you earlier if things were any better with Jenny. Sorry, I spaced it off." Jess squeezed her shoulder and pulled her closer.

"It's understandable, Jess. I left your house in a hurry." She touched his wrist. "Besides, you have a major event to consider now."

"But I'd like to be there for you when I can, especially during times like this."

Jess hit a nerve, a reminder one couldn't expect to depend on others. Her tone intensified. "But you can't. It's not possible to be with everyone for everything when the difficulties of life happen." She wiped beads of perspiration from her forehead. "We'll be fine. We've handled situations on our own since we were young and are used to it. It makes us stronger and less dependent on people."

His mouth fell open and he gripped the dress box close to his chest. "I won't interfere if you don't want my help. But I offered it since I care about you and what happens to your sister and her friend. Yes, you're strong and independent, but support can help."

With a hand on her cheek, she lowered her head. "You're right. I'm sorry, Jess. I didn't mean to be ungrateful at all. Please accept my apology. I guess I'm not handling this change as well as I thought I might. It's hard for me to face losing support once I accept it. I let my past experiences get in the way again."

"No apology necessary. It's understandable. Stressful situations are tough. I may not be here physically for a while, but I won't stop caring how you are." The slow movement of his fingers caressed her back.

Her eyes searched his. How had she come to meet such a special man? "Thanks. It means a lot."

The phone buzzed. "It's Malia. I've got to take this."

Jess stood to give her privacy.

"Yes, Malia."

"I talked to Jenny's parents. There's nothing more they can do for her. She won't regain consciousness and her organs are giving out. They'll take her off life support soon. I'm at the hospital and will wait in the lounge area outside of Jenny's room while her parents spend time alone with her."

Her heart plummeted. "I'm so sorry. I'll drive to Kahului right away and wait with you."

Malia's voice quivered. "Thanks. I appreciate it."

As Lei blinked back tears, she turned toward Jess. "They're taking Jenny off life support now. I'm heading to the hospital to wait with Malia."

"Take care. I'll be thinking about all of you." Jess embraced her. "Call me if you need to talk. I mean it."

She clung to him a moment, then pulled back and wiped tears from her cheek. "Thanks. For everything."

Inside the lobby, she hurried to pack the merchandise in her suitcase. Many of the other venders had left for the day and few people moved through the lobby during lunchtime. A convenient time to head out.

After Lei left the hotel, she drove straight to the hospital in Kahului. Inside the cool, air-conditioned hallway, she took the elevator to Jenny's floor. Past the nurses' desk, alarms rang out in patient rooms as she made her way to the visitors' lounge.

Malia sat in a chair near the window and stared downward.

"I'm here now." Lei rushed over and smoothed Malia's hair.

A sigh escaped her. "Thank heavens. I feel awful thinking how senseless this whole situation is and how poor Jenny is innocent, since the car incident was likely meant for me."

"This won't help. None of it is your fault." She sat next to Malia. "A rigged car accident shouldn't be intended for anyone. The person who planned it is the culprit."

Malia raised her head. "Jenny's been off life support for over fifty minutes. I can't imagine how her parents must feel."

"Let's offer prayers for Jenny and her parents." She folded her hands. "Dear Lord, please bring comfort, strength and peace to Jenny and her parents. We know you are with them. And help us to know how best to support them during this difficult time. In Jesus's name. Amen."

"Amen. Thank you."

They sat together holding hands and waited. A stream of light passed through the window and crept across the floor as time passed.

The door to Jenny's room opened and her parents stepped out together, arm in arm.

Lei and Malia hastened toward them.

Tears streaming down her cheeks, Jenny's mother looked at them. "She's gone. Our sweet girl has left us way too soon."

Her father's blank stare echoed his silent grief.

"I'm so terribly sorry." Malia embraced Mrs. Taylor.

Lei cradled her arms around Malia and Mrs. Taylor. The four of them stood in silence and wept.

With her head raised, Lei faced the Taylors. "Is there anything we can do? Anything at all?"

Mr. Taylor glanced at Lei. "I hope you girls will keep current with the police about this case and call them for updates. Jenny's killer needs to be brought to justice before someone else's innocent child is murdered."

Malia's voice cracked. "Absolutely. Consider it done." She took his hand. "We won't ever forget what happened or forget Jenny, you can rest assured."

The man nodded, led his wife out of the lounge and through the hallway to the elevator.

Lei faced Malia. "Will calling the police be enough? Do you think a private investigator might help if we can afford one?"

"I'll check into it for Jenny's sake and also see what her parents think later. And as Mr. Taylor said, before any other innocent victims are hurt the case needs resolution."

"For sure." Lei wiped her eyes.

"My roommate, Sara is out of town. I promised to call with any information on Jenny."

"Okay, go ahead. And I'll call Jess and let him know." She took a seat in one of the lounge chairs and punched in his number.

Jess's voice came through on the first ring. "Hi, Lei."

"I thought I'd let you know Jenny passed away." Shoulders drooped, she rubbed her aching forehead.

He lowered his voice. "I'm so sorry. How sad. I'm sure her parents are devastated. How's Malia doing?"

"As good as can be expected."

"If there's anything I can do or if you want to talk, let me know. I'll be here for another two days yet. And you can call me any time after I leave, too."

Lei sat upright. "You've made all your plans?"

"Yes, I have."

"Tell me. I'd like to know, and I can definitely use a distraction right now, too."

"After I arrive and stay a night in the hotel, I'll meet with Eva Rose the next day for a short visit along with Paula at her home. The paternity and DNA tests are under way for Eva Rose right now. We'll also spend some time sorting out details for future visitation and our communication, depending how these short visits work out."

"Great. It sounds like everything is all set up for you. I wish you the best. I should go now, Jess."

She slipped the phone in her purse and walked over to Malia. "Let's leave. We can talk at your apartment for a while if you want. Maybe think things over about resolving the case and help keep our minds off how awful we feel about Jenny."

"Yeah, good idea."

They left the visitors lounge and headed for Malia's apartment. As Lei turned onto the dusty road, lined by a small field of waving sugarcane, questions flooded her mind. So much happened today. Jess would leave soon. Poor Jenny passed away.

And then the grieving Taylors, who wanted the person responsible for Jenny's death apprehended for justice and the sake of others.

Could Lei truly help? Where did she fit into all of these issues? With no idea and little to no control over them, she needed direction and all the prayers she could muster.

CHAPTER FOURTEEN

The view from the Iowa hotel window revealed rows of cornfields. A little over a day ago Jess flew over the few sugarcane fields of Maui. Dissimilar worlds, but not as different as the family dynamic he would soon encounter.

The hotel location worked great for him. The highway nearby led right into town for his visit with Eva Rose, and also to his mother's home in the opposite direction.

He picked up the photos of Eva Rose from the bedside table and viewed them again. Staying so close to his daughter made their meeting all the more real to him, no longer only a dream.

Caught up on his rest from the jet lag, maybe he'd call Lei before venturing out this afternoon, since he couldn't see Eva Rose until tomorrow. Sitting on the bed, he tapped his fingers on the bedside table and waited for her to answer. One ring. Two rings.

"Hello, Jess. How was your trip?"

"Good. Right on time. I realize it's early there, but I had a chance to call."

"It's okay. I'm up and am going back to work this morning."

"How are you and how is Malia doing, considering?"

"Pretty good. After the funeral, we talked with Jenny's parents. They decided to hire a private investigator, something Malia and I had discussed earlier. I think it'll help Malia and Jenny's parents focus on finding the perpetrator and hoping to keep others from harm."

It was so good to hear her voice. He relaxed back on the bed. "It's an excellent idea."

"When will you see Eva Rose?"

"Tomorrow. I should let you know the results came back from the DNA paternity. I checked online and I am her biological father without a doubt."

Her voice rose. "It's good you have the verification now."

"Yes. I think I'll take a drive and give my mom a visit later to let her know what's going on, especially since there's definite proof I'm Eva Rose's father now."

"Good idea. It sounds like a great start, having things settled with your mom today, so you can focus on your visit with Eva Rose tomorrow."

How fortunate he had Lei in his life. She cared so much. "I'll call you again. Feel free to call me, too. I'm five hours ahead of you with the time zone difference." He paused. "Remember, I care about you and think of you often."

Her voice cracked. "Me, too. I'll be thinking about all of you there."

Jess ended the call and tapped a fist against his lips. He wanted Lei, wanted his daughter and also a specially planned career. Too much to expect? He prayed he wouldn't hurt anyone along the way. Hadn't Lei said we couldn't be there for everyone and everything despite our efforts?

If he sat in the hotel room any longer, he'd go mad. Jess texted his mother, left the hotel and headed for the silver Camry in the parking lot he'd rented. He shoved his sunglasses on and drove off the premises, but he didn't turn in the direction toward his mother's house.

Maybe he'd made a mistake, but the urge to drive by Paula's home seized him. He wouldn't stop or stare, but he wanted to see the residence where she and his daughter lived.

As he drove through the tree-lined streets on the beautiful sunny day, his heart rate increased as he approached the house.

Jess turned onto Circle Terrace. He glanced at the house numbers and looked for number 716.

A large, two-story brick home with white columns showed the numbers in black by the door. He drew in a shallow breath and a trickle of sweat ran down the side of his face. No one in the yard. But he could imagine his daughter hopping up the brick steps to the entryway of the house.

Driving to the end of the street, Jess made a right turn and headed toward the highway. He exhaled as he drove toward his mother's home. All the years he'd hoped and waited to find Eva Rose made it surreal to accept his dream would happen tomorrow. Only one more day away.

Forty-five minutes later, he parked in the driveway of Mom's house as he'd done so many times before. Lots of memories surfaced here, both good and some challenging. He walked along the curved sidewalk next to the freshly mown lawn and rapped on the door.

Jess opened it and poked his head inside the house. "Mom, it's me."

Mom's heels clicked on the wooden floor and she came into view. With her brown hair tied back and thin brows raised, her green eyes sparkled when she caught sight of him.

"Welcome home, Jess." She opened her arms wide.

He hurried toward her and enveloped her petite frame with a tight hug. "Mom, it's so good to see you."

Mom glanced up at him. "I happened to make one of your favorites for dinner. You will stay, won't you?"

"Of course. When have I ever turned down one of your delicious, home-cooked meals?"

The corners of her mouth turned up and she sat on the cocoa-brown sofa. "Come have a seat. I want to hear everything."

Jess hoped so. The subject of the Jules family's past in relation to Jess had proved difficult for her and his father many times over the years. He glanced at the well-used, leather recliner where Dad used to sit, but sat across from Mom in the crème, wing back chair. "I haven't heard from the company I hope will hire me on Oahu yet, so I'll remain at my current security job for a while. When it ends, I'll look for another temporary position if I haven't heard from the employer in Honolulu."

Mom pressed an index finger to her chin. "Sounds reasonable. It's all well and good. But do tell me about the young woman you're seeing. I hope your relationship is going well."

Their complications were best left unsaid. Mom would hear enough tonight. "We've enjoyed the time we spent together. But she's dealt with two losses and funerals recently, and I've planned this trip, so time's been tight for us. Remind me later. I have some hand-made gifts from Lei in the trunk and something I picked up for you."

"How nice of both of you." Mom leaned forward. "I'm glad you're together yet. It's a good sign. You know I can't wait forever to see you married and give me grandchildren."

Jess clutched his hands together and bit his bottom lip. She had a seven-year-old granddaughter. Once he told her the truth, what would Mom say regarding Eva Rose? "You're getting a bit ahead of yourself with the wedding bells, but you're well aware of it." He pointed his index finger toward her.

Mom's beaming face flushed with color. "I do know, but I'm your mother. I'm not getting any younger and most importantly, I want you to have the life you deserve."

Jess held his palms out. "Okay. Enough said."

"What else do you have to tell me?" Mom sat up straight and stared at him.

The moment had arrived. "I've told you a big part of this visit has to do with the Jules family and Mr. Jules passing away." His chest tightened.

"I remember the old story too well." Mom's brows squeezed together. "What else about them would bring you back?"

He squeezed his eyes shut a moment and drew in a breath. *Just say it.* "Since his death I have located Paula. We've been in communication and—"

Mom jolted forward and her voice soared. "But why would you take up with her? You said it was over."

"It is, Mom. I'm not here for Paula, but for Eva Rose." He challenged her tone. "Yes, it's her name. Eva Rose."

Mom crossed her arms and looked away from him. "Well I would expect Paula gave the child a name, for heaven's sake."

His body temperature rose and his jaw tightened. "Look at me, Mom."

She faced him. "All right. I'm listening."

He folded his hands to keep from fidgeting. "We've had paternity testing done recently. I'm Eva Rose's father. It's certain she is my daughter."

Mom's jaw dropped and she tilted her head to the side. "What does it mean for you? What will you do?"

"I'll legally be Eva Rose's father. I'm planning to meet her tomorrow. I hope in time she'll get to know me and want to spend time in my life." He paused. "And in yours. Regardless of what the future holds for all of us, she is your granddaughter."

Mom pressed hands against her temples and the cords in her throat protruded. "I-I don't know what to say."

His voice rose. "Believe me, I totally understand. It's a big deal, but these are the facts."

Mom's gaze darted back and forth and she blew out a noisy breath. "I have to let this sink in for a bit."

"Yes, it'll take time." He rubbed his palms together. Mom had chosen to believe all along Eva Rose wasn't his child. The news hadn't shaken her as much as he thought it might. Not yet, anyway. "I'll let you go see to dinner for a few minutes if you want, while I go retrieve the gifts from the trunk for you."

"Yes, of course. Dinner." Mom stood and nodded.

"But first I want to show you a photo of Eva Rose." Jess strode over to his mother.

She stared at him, wide-eyed. "You have a picture of her?"

Jess pulled out his wallet. "Yes, several." He handed them to her. "These are your copies to keep."

Mom's hand trembled as she took hold of them and studied each one. She placed fingers to her upper lip and her eyes watered.

"Oh, Jess, she's beautiful. Such a lovely child. I only wish." Mom paused. "I wish your father could've been here."

Tears ran down his cheeks as he hugged his mother. "Me, too, Mom. Me, too."

Jess couldn't remember when he'd had such a moment of closeness with his mother. Now, he prayed he might get through the rest of this night and have the strength necessary for his meeting with Paula and Eva Rose tomorrow, whatever it brought.

*

The next morning, Jess arrived at Paula's home a few minutes early. He sat in the car and his hands gripped the steering wheel, unable to fully believe he would truly meet his daughter in a few minutes.

He drew in a breath, picked up the sack with the gifts for his child, climbed the brick steps to the door and knocked.

The door opened. There stood Paula who looked much like she had more than seven years ago, tall with sandy, brown hair and blue eyes.

"Come in, Jess."

He stepped inside the door and placed the package on the floor. His voice cracked. "How've you been, Paula?"

"Quite well, thank you."

How formal they conducted themselves. Jess would've hugged her, but somehow it didn't seem appropriate now. He extended his palms to Paula. She placed her hands in his and their eyes locked. The years melted away a moment for Jess as he looked into his past at the mother of his child. "It's so good of you to have invited me. I've looked forward to it."

Paula stepped across the silvery carpet and motioned toward two black leather sofas facing each other near the fireplace. "Please have a seat. I thought we'd chat for a while before you meet Eva Rose. We can get some of the details out of the way we need to discuss and then focus on our daughter."

Our daughter. Unbelievable. "Okay. Good idea." He sat on the edge of the couch.

Paula sat across from him on the opposite sofa. "Now with the paternity confirmed, what else is on your mind?"

Everything and anything. Slipping his hands into his pockets, he tapped his heel against the carpet. *Say this correctly.* "First of all, I want you to know I plan on paying child support. Whether you want to run it through legal channels or make a suggestion how to handle it, I'll listen."

Her head tilted. "It's not an issue for me. My father left Eva Rose and me well taken care of, financially."

"Nevertheless, I feel the responsibility to help however I can. And maybe start a fund for college, too."

Paula's eyes softened. "As you wish. It's entirely up to you."

"Fine." Jess cleared his throat, never so nervous in his life. "The next question is the handling of future visits. Right now, I plan on staying in Hawaii. I finished a special investigation certification and am waiting for an opening for a position on Oahu. I can provide and do the best there, versus anything around this area. But I know the distance makes it more difficult. However, I'm open to moving back to this area if works better. In the meantime, maybe we can call and use laptops to communicate."

"Eva Rose is too young for much social media and Internet in my opinion, but I'll let her see emails you send her and consider buying her a phone I can manage and monitor so you can call her, depending on how things go after the visit today."

He rubbed sweaty palms on his thighs. Depending. Another reminder this visit might turn from a dream into a nightmare. "Okay, sure. It sounds like a good beginning." Anything was better than nothing.

Paula's head tilted to the side. "How often do you expect you'd want to come here and visit her, Jess?"

He rubbed his palms back and forth. "As often as I can afford it and have the time to get away. From Hawaii, a general estimate might be a couple of times a year or so. It'll depend on my work situation and finances, too. It's up in the air for now."

"Okay. Perfectly understandable."

But he wanted to see his daughter more often or for longer periods of time. "I'd like to hope Eva Rose would come for a visit in the summer or maybe during school breaks once we become acquainted in due time."

Paula's eyes widened. "Eva Rose can't travel alone. Surely you understand."

"Yes, of course I do." His voice lowered and he fidgeted with his hands. "Would it be possible for you to accompany her on the trip over to Hawaii?"

She folded her arms across her chest and glanced away. "It's hard to say. I don't know."

Jess didn't want to push Paula away before he even met his daughter. "Right. I'm thinking a bit too far ahead. I understand you have a life here and other obligations."

"I don't work outside of the home and I do have the time and resources, so those aren't issues."

What then? "It's none of my business. Sorry, I shouldn't have asked."

Paula moved forward. "Jess. I've been seeing someone and it's become serious. In time, I will have someone else to consider besides myself and Eva Rose."

Jess glanced downward. "I see. Yes, it makes a difference." He didn't know what else to say, yet he understood relationships with others made the situation more complicated as he and Lei had learned.

Her voice softened. "What about you? Anyone special?"

"After all these years, I do have someone special now." He pictured Lei in his head.

Paula tipped her head to the side. "Is she likely to stick around? I only ask for Eva Rose's sake. The people we bring into our personal lives affect her. And if she gets to know them and they suddenly leave, it makes it even more difficult for her."

"Yeah, it makes sense. Of course, I'd like to think the relationship would move forward, but I don't have a solid answer for you today. Lei is from Maui, has a home, a new business and isn't interested in moving anywhere else. I may move to Oahu, possibly soon. Or elsewhere. I don't know how the move will affect our relationship. I will update you in time."

"Okay. I'll keep it in mind. Are you ready to meet your daughter now?"

Jess's heart thundered at the thought. He'd been wrong earlier when he said he'd never been more nervous. "Yes, but first tell me. Is there anything I should or shouldn't say?"

"No, Jess. I've told her your name, and she knows you're her birth father so it's a good start."

Paula left the room and Jess brought the sack of gifts back to the couch with him.

He dug in his pocket and took out his phone so he'd remember to take a photograph with Eva Rose if Paula didn't mind. His breaths shallow, heat surged through him. Where were the two of them? Did Eva Rose decide she didn't want to meet him at the last minute?

Paula smiled as she entered the living room area holding Eva Rose's hand. She glanced at him with a shy grin and placed a finger on her chin. He'd never seen anyone so beautiful as his child in his entire life.

Breathless, with a racing pulse, Jess stepped over to Eva Rose and squatted to her level. "Hi, Eva Rose. I'm Jess, your dad. I'm so happy to meet you."

Eva Rose's soft voice melted him. "Hi, Jess. Daddy."

Jess wanted to pick her up, kiss her and twirl her around, but didn't dare. He returned to the sofa and held up the sack. "I've brought you several things from Hawaii, where I live."

The child glanced up at Paula.

"Honey, go pick one from the sack and open it. It's enough for right now."

The girl edged toward Jess. He opened the sack, and she pulled out a box.

When she opened it, her eyes widened. The menehune dress Lei had made grabbed Eva Rose's attention. "This is pretty. What are the little men?"

His daughter asked him a question. "You've heard of leprechauns, right?"

Eva Rose's beautiful hair slid along her cheeks as she nodded her head.

144

"They're the kind of leprechauns we have in Hawaii and they're called menehunes."

Eva Rose couldn't contain a grin and held the dress up to her body. "Thank you."

"You're more than welcome, Eva Rose." His insides turned to mush.

Eva Rose turned and faced her mother. "I want to try it on, Mom."

"Go ahead, honey." Paula returned to the sofa and sat across from him.

Jess watched her dance her way out of the living room. He folded his hands to keep them calm. "This meant the world to me, Paula. Thank you so much."

Her eyes searched his. "She's your child, too."

His child. A bond. "Would you take our picture when Eva Rose returns?"

"Of course."

"I'd like to come visit again before I have to leave, since I don't know when I'll be able to return again. But it's up to you. Whatever you think is best for her."

"I think it's a good idea." Paula raised a brow. "It's hard to tell from one short visit how she'll ultimately handle this. Let's see how another visit goes for her."

Jess had hoped for more than one visit in the back of his head, but now he rejoiced at the opportunity of seeing her again. Could this day get any better?

His daughter returned wearing the dress. How precious. He couldn't wait to show Lei the photo of Eva Rose wearing the menehune outfit.

"Eva Rose, can we take a few pictures?" Jess held his phone up in the air.

"Yeah."

"Okay. Ready?" He snapped two, then Paula took one of him with Eva Rose.

He faced his daughter. "It's time for me to go. But I had a great time today with you."

Eva Rose smiled at him.

Jess walked to the door, not wanting to leave. "I'll see you again soon, Eva Rose. You, too, Paula. Thanks for everything."

Paula nodded.

Jess closed the door behind him and drew in a deep breath.

Fifteen minutes later, he sat in the chair of his hotel room, mentally flying from the visit with his child, Eva Rose. His. An urge to share this special moment with Lei overwhelmed him.

He punched in the number. An answer on the first ring.

"How is everything, Jess?"

"Absolutely wonderful. I get to have another visit with Eva Rose before I leave, too. I'll send you a photo of me with her in the dress you made her. It fit perfectly."

Jess described the details of the entire visit to her, all the while barely taking in a breath.

"It's fantastic news. I'm so happy for both of you."

He leaned forward in the chair. "Now tell me how you're doing and what's happened since I've been gone."

"I'm doing okay." She hesitated. "I do have a piece of news."

He pressed the phone closer to his ear. "I'm listening."

"Remember I told you about the private investigator Jenny's parents hired?"

"Yes."

"Recently someone rigged a car leading to an accident and a man was apprehended for it. The driver wasn't hurt, but the police and an investigator figured out who might've been responsible and they traced it to a mechanic."

He sat up straight and his voice rose. "Do they think he's the same guy who cut Malia's car brakes?"

"We don't know for sure. He has an alibi of sorts, but the investigator is watching him closely and digging into his background. Hopefully, we'll know more soon."

"It'd be great if it's a link, so they can resolve Jenny's case as well as keep the man from harming others, too."

"Exactly. Let's hope so." She paused. "When will you be back?"

Did she miss him like he missed her? "In a few days. I'll call you before I leave."

"I pray your next meeting with Eva Rose goes as well as the first."

"Thanks. Me, too."

Jess heaved out a breath. Where to go from here with future visitation? Since meeting Eva Rose, he would never let her go. But would seeing her a couple of times a year be enough, especially to have adequate time to bond with him? Eva Rose had to adjust to the man in Paula's life, too, who would see his daughter more often than Jess did.

He imagined Lei, Malia and Jenny's parents experienced a little helplessness, as he did, with their hands tied, waiting and worrying. In Jenny's case they could only hope and pray for a resolution before someone else got hurt. And with Eva Rose, the time he spent with her would be limited to some extent, no matter where he lived, a fact out of his control. And what about his relationship with Lei?

So many unanswered questions for all of them. But he'd make the effort to resolve them as best as possible.

*

Two days later, Jess sat on Paula's sofa again, this time seated next to Eva Rose.

Paula sat across from them and gazed at Jess. "I'm glad we were able to have all the legal papers signed while you were here."

"Me, too. I'm glad you requested the forms be prepared ahead of time, especially since I'll leave tomorrow morning. Thanks for everything, Paula. I'll keep you posted if I happen to move, and on what's happening in my life, which might involve the three of us." Jess placed his arm around Eva Rose, who studied the new phone her mother had given her.

"Sounds good. Eva Rose and I were glad to have you visit. Have a safe trip, Jess."

Eva Rose faced Jess. "Daddy, would you put your number in my phone so I can call you?"

Hearing her voice even melted his heart. "Of course, honey. I'll do it and then I have to leave."

Her eyes widened. "Already? You just got here a little while ago."

A heaviness in his chest gripped him, and his heart ached for his little girl. "I know, Eva Rose. But we had a good time while I was here. I loved seeing your room and playing with you on your swing set. I wish I could stay, but I have to go back to work and it's a long trip home."

She handed him the phone and stared downward.

Nothing about this situation was Eva Rose's fault. He blinked back tears while he finished adding his contact number into the phone. "Here you go, Eva Rose. Now you can call me when it's okay with your mom. I'll look forward to hearing all about you and everything you do."

Her small hand reached for the phone. "Okay, Daddy Jess."

"Can I have a hug, sweetie?" He pushed the bangs out of her eyes.

"Yeah." Eva Rose's arms flung wide open.

Jess held his child close in his arms for the first time, and wished he could hold her forever. "I love you, Eva Rose."

She spoke into his ear. "I love you too, Daddy."

He finally let her go.

When the doorbell chimed, Paula answered it. A tall, dark-haired man wearing an expensive-looking black suit stepped inside and hugged Paula.

They walked to the sofa across from Jess. Paula extended her arm toward the man. "Jess, this is my friend, Michael Finn."

Eva Rose hopped off the sofa and ran toward Michael and Paula.

Michael extended his hand.

Jess reached over and shook it. "I'm Jess Park. Nice to meet you."

Eva Rose tugged at Michael's pant leg. "Daddy Mike. I missed you."

He took her hand in his. "I missed you too, sweetheart."

Jess's shoulders slumped, and he faced Paula. "Thanks for your hospitality. I'll be leaving now."

Paula stepped toward him. "I'll see you to the door."

A little choked up, Jess glanced at her. "Please, you have company. I can see myself out."

He walked toward the door and listened to his daughter giggle and converse with Michael. He had to get out of there before he lost it altogether in front of all of them.

Jess opened the door and caught a quick glimpse of the three of them together, all smiles as he left.

They were a family and Jess appreciated it for Eva Rose's sake. But Jess remained an outsider. He shouldn't think such a thing, yet his feelings said so at this moment.

He entered the car, took a deep breath and remembered his fortunate opportunity to meet his daughter. But was this situation fair to her? He understood Eva Rose needed a stable family life, yet he was her biological father.

Should he more seriously consider moving back to the mainland whether he could afford it or not?

He and Paula led different lives now. Even if he did return, he wouldn't have the opportunity to live with his daughter on a day-to-day basis and needed to drill the fact into his head.

Logic and emotions played a cruel, conflicting game in his mind. Jess never faced an emotional roller coaster like this one, determining what might be best for everyone and considering a decision based on what his own emotions told him he wanted, namely his child.

He prayed he'd come to understand what was best for Eva Rose. The ultimate decision should depend on her needs.

CHAPTER FIFTEEN

A yawn escaped Lei as she sat at the kitchen table with the laptop and scrolled through the email. Three days had passed since talking with Jess. He'd stayed longer on the mainland than she'd anticipated and wondered if it meant good news for him or not. In the meantime, keeping busy with work and volunteering at the school helped keep her mind off him.

A closer look at one of the email addresses caught her attention. Her half-sister Catherine Hudson sent a reply.

Dearest Lei,

I am so glad you contacted me. Dad told me about the three of you when I was young. While some of the stories he shared were happy ones, I could see the sorrow in his eyes when he spoke about all of you.

Tears tumbled down her cheeks. Their father hadn't totally forgotten them and maybe even cared about them.

I'm sorry I have to tell you he wasn't able to spend much time with me before he passed away. Unfortunately, drugs won the battle against him. He tried several times to stop the habit, but he couldn't manage it in the end. I think Dad cared for all of us with the best of his ability. I was in grade school when he died. If you want to share any information or correspond, it is fine with me. I would love to hear from you and get to know you better. I have no other siblings, so was pleased to hear an update about you, Malia and Kimo. And if you'd like, maybe someday we can meet.

      Your sister,
      Catherine

Lei pinched the bridge of her nose and closed her eyes for a moment. After years of hurt and mixed feelings, had she dealt with her father's absence the wrong way? Now, a whole different perspective of him came to light.

She opened the attachment of the photo. Catherine had blue eyes and light brown hair like their father, unlike the three of them, who inherited the ebony hair and eyes of their Hawaiian mother. With the email forwarded to Malia, she'd share the news with Jess later. This was another one of those times God took a hard situation in life and made something good occur from it.

Lei, Malia and Kimo were separated when they'd entered the many years in the foster care system, but they'd had some time together beforehand and a little since they'd become adults. How difficult and lonely it must've been for Catherine when their father was out of the picture, with her having no siblings. Yes, she would answer Catherine later.

After closing the laptop, she headed to the hotel with a box of clothes in the trunk. The afternoon sun beat down on her as she carried the container of men's used clothing from the car into the Hawaiian Hotel. Beads of perspiration trickled down her neck while entering the storage room near the lobby. She found an open space on a table and hurried to set the heavy cardboard receptacle on it. Pastor Kane should arrive any time now to distribute them to the needy later.

Out of the storage room, she breezed through the lobby past the purple dendrobium orchid display and left the building. Pastor Kane sat in the shade of an enormous kukui tree behind the lava rock waterfall.

She waved, and he motioned her to join him. They sat next to each other on a wooden bench.

"Pastor, the storage room is quite full. Do you want me to help fill the church van?"

"No thanks. I'm waiting for a few young men to help load the clothes and then deliver them. We'll stop at the jail, too. People leaving there often need something to start out with, or wear to job interviews, that sort of thing."

"Then my grandmother's great-nephew, Dirk's clothes should help. You met him at the memorial and scattering of her ashes."

He scratched his chin. "Ah, yes. I remember him. Nice dresser. The men will be thrilled."

She tucked a wisp of her hair behind her ear. "I collected lots of casual clothes, too, but he donated mostly dress clothes."

"Wonderful." He sat up straight. "And tell me, how's Kimo doing?"

Her tone increased. "Dirk says Kimo has found a job."

"Good." Pastor Kane glanced at her. "And you?"

She folded her arms and glanced downward. "I'm fine. Busy at work and enjoying my home."

"I haven't heard you mention Jess in a while and haven't seen him with you at church services lately."

Lei let out a huge breath and gazed up at the pastor. Maybe she did need to talk about Jess. "He's on the mainland visiting his seven-year-old daughter he recently located, for a first time visit."

His eyes widened. "My goodness. What an emotional time it must be for him and his daughter. How do you feel about it?"

"I couldn't be happier for him."

Pastor leaned closer to her. "Yes, but I asked how you felt about this, in your relationship with him. You seem a little down today."

"A child comes first, in my opinion." Her chin quivered. "I need to understand and accept it might be the end of our relationship. He could move back to the mainland. I'm not part of the situation and so am dealing with it the best way I know how."

He raised an index finger. "You mean the way which hasn't truly worked for you before, closing off the circumstances or persons involved to hide the pain? I see people end up in addictions, seek revenge, find themselves in jail or worse, since they don't deal with life issues and let the pain go. It's easier to go to drugs, or whatever soothes a person for the moment. It's not easy for them to change, but they need to trust in God enough to help them deal with their hurts to move forward. I'm not saying you're like these people at all, but I don't want to see you shut down and bury this inside."

Her pitch heightened. "I don't want the emotional pain again."

The pastor tilted his head to the side. "But aren't you already hurt? What's more, you've made the decision on your own before Jess even returns. You say you're not part of the situation, but aren't you? Sometimes we have to go through suffering to understand afterwards what true joy means. Then we can grow as a person and make better choices in life. Maybe help others the way we needed help once."

Tears trickled down her cheek. "Do you honestly think there's hope for me to change and overcome these fears?"

"Yes, of course. You've come a long way." He tapped her on the shoulder. "Pray to be strong and make the effort to change your thinking about this for the better. Have faith and believe it."

She wiped away the tears from her face. "You know people who have done this and are better for it?"

His eyes widened. "Of course I do. I know another pastor who had a terrible childhood. He married and gave his children what he didn't have. He could've shut down and cut people out of his life after what he went through, but he didn't, you see."

Two men approached the pastor.

Lei breathed easier. "Pastor, you've been a great help. Thank you."

She walked to the parking lot and headed for home. At first she didn't want to hear it, but Pastor Kane made a lot of sense. Yet much of her future with Jess depended on his decisions, didn't they? Okay, it's what she'd wanted to believe. She had choices, too.

As soon as she turned into the driveway, the phone played its tune. Malia.

"Hi, Lei. I wanted to let you know the latest."

"I hope it's good news." Lei walked into the house, dropped her purse on the counter and sat at the kitchen table.

"Yeah, I think so. Jenny's mother called me. The police department is questioning the man I told you about, the one likely related to Jenny's case. It's possible they have linked him to yet another case with a rigged vehicle. The private investigator said the guy used to be a mechanic, but is currently out of work, which might explain why he took unethical jobs."

She tapped her fingers on the table. "Hmm. Interesting. Sounds suspicious, doesn't it?"

"Yeah. The hope is they can eventually find out if the same person or people hired him. But they have to find out much more, with the intention to press further charges upon him and then he might be more agreeable to talk or make a plea deal."

"Wow." Lei sat upright, taking in all the information. "Thanks for letting me know."

"Have you heard anything from Jess?"

She squeezed the back of her neck, wondering why he hadn't called yet. "Not since he first arrived on the mainland. He said he'd call me before he headed home. It should be any time now. He has to return to work soon."

"I'm sure you miss him."

She squeezed her eyes shut a moment, not ready to talk about her relationship with Jess. "Yes, Malia, I do. Thanks for calling. I'll talk to you later."

With the phone placed on the table, she leaned back in the chair a moment and hoped the leads in the case would come together. A few minutes later the phone buzzed again, and she scrambled to grab it.

"Hey, there. It's Jess."

Lei jerked forward, her spine as straight as a pole. She hadn't checked the caller ID. "Hello, Jess. It's so good to hear your voice."

"I'm heading to the airport tomorrow, early in the morning. I'll be back later in the day Hawaii time. After I unpack and get caught up on jet lag, I'll give you a call."

Her breath caught and a flush of heat coursed through her body. "Okay. I'll be waiting. I'm anxious to talk with you." She wanted to ask him so many questions.

"Great, me too. And I can't wait to see you."

Her brows gathered. "Jess, did everything continue to work out the way you hoped?"

"It's getting late here and I need to drive to Mom's yet and talk with her. There's too much to convey over the phone anyway. I'd rather tell you everything in person."

"Sure. Okay. See you soon. Have a safe trip home."

With the call ended, her mind raced in circles. How much could he have to tell her? Were there decisions made he didn't want her to know about ahead of time before they met? Did things change after the first visit with Eva Rose he didn't like? Could Lei find contentment without Jess in her life if necessary? She had to stop this. Guessing or making assumptions didn't help matters at all.

A chill ran up her spine. She left the kitchen, looked out the window at the hibiscus hedge toward Jess's house, walked into the living room and flopped down on the couch.

He'd come home tomorrow night. And soon thereafter, the truth about his visit and all of their futures more evident. Now to gain the strength and faith to deal with whatever came her way.

CHAPTER SIXTEEN

Two mornings later, Lei hooked up the hose at the side of the house. It hadn't rained and the heat took its toll on some of the plants in the yard. She glanced past the hibiscus bushes into Jess's yard. No word from him yet.

The water spray hissed as she doused the red ti leaf and the jasmine plants. She yanked the hose along and rounded the corner to the back of the house. Stopping dead in her tracks, she shut off the sprayer and stared at the clods of freshly overturned soil in the same area someone had unearthed beforehand.

Her heart raced. Not again. Lei dropped the hose, took in a few shallow breaths and stepped closer. Maybe a dog was to blame this time. No, the old rock wall showed again, so the hole was deeper than she'd first thought. A quick survey of the backyard didn't show any other signs of mischief near the hole. After a glance upward, her jaw dropped open. The newly installed camera at the roof's edge skewed the opposite way from its usual position.

Her scalp prickled. She shouldn't make negative assumptions. It was probably nothing but two separate incidents. No major harm done, no one hurt. Her fists opened and closed. Remain calm.

She picked up the hose, returned to the other side of the house and shut off the water valve before going inside the house. When did it happen? She stopped in the kitchen at the sink and rinsed her hands. Maybe while at Malia's last evening.

A quick view of the camera video would reveal if or when the camera might've been moved or show the time when it moved sideways. She sat on the sofa in the living room and took in a few deep breaths. Odd as the occurrence was, she was fine and needed to keep things in perspective. Nothing major happened, as with Jenny's accident. Yes, she'd made too much of it.

The phone rang, and she jolted from the sofa. Jess.

"Hey, Lei. I'd like to see you if you have the time."

Her stomach fluttered. "I sure do. Welcome back. Come on in and I'll have coffee poured for you."

Lei hurried into the kitchen, took out another mug and filled it along with her own. She placed the steaming coffee cups on the table.

The screen door opened, and she ran to Jess. He squeezed her with a bear hug and his lips met hers, slow with a long kiss. She ran her hands through his hair and his aftershave filled her nostrils. Her Jess.

"Oh, Jess. It's so good to see you and be close to you again."

He pulled back with his hands on her shoulders and gazed into her eyes. "I feel the same way. I've missed you so much."

She extended her palm toward the table. "Sit down, please. Have some coffee and tell me everything."

Jess pulled out a chair and picked up the coffee mug. "Whoa. It's a tall order for me to tell everything. I'll give it a try as long as you promise to fill me in on what's happened since we last spoke."

"Okay. It's a deal." She stared at the table and remembered the camera.

"I'll save the daddy pictures and praise about Eva Rose for later." He took a swig of his brew. "Mm. I've missed your great Kona coffee, too."

Hands folded on the table, she smiled. "Whatever you want to share is fine."

He glanced downward. "Overall, I'm satisfied with the time we spent together."

Something didn't set well with him. She tipped her head to the side. "Except what, Jess?"

He exhaled. "Paula said after the last meeting Eva Rose seemed a little confused about who I am in her life and who Michael is, since she has also spent some time with him. In reality, much more time than I have spent with her."

She squinted. "Who is Michael?"

"Oh." His head jerked back. "He will likely be Paula's fiancé soon. While I was visiting, Paula told me they were serious and considering marriage. He's fairly new in Eva Rose's life and I'm totally new, so you can imagine the two big adjustments for her all at once and how we might fit into her life. Right now it's a hard question to answer. Eva Rose knows I'm her biological father and Michael might become her stepfather. But it doesn't address how she feels or relates to us yet."

"Where does all this leave you for spending time with her?"

"With my current circumstances, I can go visit a few times a year, email through Paula and call Eva Rose."

How difficult this must be for Jess. "And you're okay with it?"

His brows rose. "I have to be. If I push, Eva Rose could get upset, and Paula might have concerns and need for our daughter to back off a while. We don't want such a situation. And we'd rather not go through lawyers and certainly no legal battles. Eva Rose has enough adjustments to make. It's the best I can do for now, especially given our distance and my wallet. Anything is better than nothing."

For now. Had he changed his work plans? "What about your security job at the hotel and the Oahu employment prospect?" She swallowed a large gulp of the coffee and it burned her throat.

He let out a sigh and caught her gaze. "The hotel has nothing more for me after I cover some vacations. They said they'd email me while I was gone, if they did have more work for me. Either I keep working at positions which pay little and scrimp by, or eventually try the few other cities which provide the type of position I've trained for, like the one on Oahu. If the company in Honolulu doesn't contact me, it would mean applying to another large city. Los Angeles and New York would have the most positions available. None of them are in Eva Rose's backyard and also far away from here. But with a less paying position I can't afford much period, let alone pay for travel thousands of miles away on a routine basis." He sipped more of the coffee.

She leaned in, her tone gentle. "I can't imagine how tough these decisions must be for you."

"A lot of it's out of my control." Jess ran a hand through his hair, his gaze distant. "Pray and hope for the best. One thing I can do is to scout around for some work soon for the time being and decide if it's worth my waiting for the Oahu position or considering something elsewhere."

Lei rose, her body tense as she gripped the coffee pot. "Let me give you a refill." Not knowing what else to say, she poured the brew for him. Hearing the situation from his side made her understand what a difficult quandary he faced. She had an excellent job and a home and only herself to consider. How unfair to wish he would stay on Maui, but she couldn't help it at times.

Jess blew across the cup of steaming Kona. "Now I want to hear what's gone on in your life since I left."

She returned to her seat. "Nothing more on the mechanic yet, but they're working on finding out what more they can. Malia mentioned she had heard nothing from Eric since before the car accident, when he last showed up here, angry about her driving by his home. I haven't heard a peep from him since then, either. I have my doubts whether he's involved, but there's no proof of anything yet."

"We'll know more in time. I would think they'd get more out of the mechanic guy once they dig deeper and find more charges on him or maybe question him at a hearing if they get enough evidence."

She swallowed the last of the coffee, pressed her lips into a thin line and shifted in the chair, not wanting to bother him with the digging in the backyard again. "Kimo has a job and is getting by until he receives his inheritance. He's staying with Dirk in the meantime. Elle has a job, too. It's all the family news I have."

"Don't tell me it's all the news you have." He squinted, his arms tight against his body. "I know you well enough to see something's bothering you. Let's have it right now."

"All right, fine." She pushed the mug away from her. "Something loosened the dirt around the rocky area in the backyard where someone previously dug."

Jess placed his palms on the table and stood. "What? I hope you called the police."

"No, I haven't yet." Her jaw twitched. "I found it right before you came. Probably happened last evening when I left home and spent time with Malia."

His voice rose. "You need to call them now."

Lowering her elbows onto the table, she sighed and pressed her hands against her temples. "I'll do it real soon."

"Did the camera show anything?"

"I haven't looked at the last of the recording yet." Her hands trembled. "The camera in the backyard was twisted sideways."

"Are you kidding me?" Jess rushed to her side. "This is serious. Someone is stalking the area for a reason."

*

A few hours later, Jess closed his laptop after his search for job opportunities. With lunch finished, he put his hands on the edge of the table and pushed his chair back. The repeated incidents at Lei's house stumped him. Absolutely bizarre. Time to check if the police had finished their investigation at her home. He tapped in the number.

"Have the police left?"

"Yes."

Jess stood and looked out the window toward her house. "What did they say?"

"They looked around and found part of a footprint near where the dirt was upturned, but nothing else. It's a large one, likely a man's."

"It's something, anyway." He ran a hand through his hair. "I bought some wire, cage-like material to cover the site if you want me to put it over the entire area. I can dig deeper around the area first, if you want to see if there's something else we can find, too."

"All right, if you don't mind."

"What did the camera show?" He turned and headed out the door.

"A man, they think, who wore a hood and had his face covered, of course. Then it blacked out when he discovered the camera and turned it. As I suspected, the time showed it happened while I was at Malia's lasts night."

"I'm on my way over right now."

Jess shoved the phone in his pocket, opened his tin shed and took the wire, a shovel and a small tool bag. Carrying them into Lei's backyard, he glanced at the camera, now pointed back in the proper place. He turned and saw her standing nearby.

"Shouldn't take me long to dig around this small space." Jess pulled his white T-shirt over his head and tossed it on the wire caging. He shoveled the red soil away from the lava rock semi-circle wall. Sweat trickled down his neck and back. "There doesn't seem to be anything around this wall. I can dig a little deeper."

She stepped closer to him. "No. You've done enough. If something is way down there, a person would need more than a shovel to find it. I found out the wall isn't ancient, so the digging shouldn't have anything to do with it."

He took his T-shirt, ran it across his forehead and tucked it in the side of his jeans. "Good to know. It tells us there's another reason someone is digging. I'll put in the fence after I shovel the dirt back in place."

"Thanks so much for doing this." She brought him the wire. "It's not quite the welcome home I hoped for you, however. You have my back every time something happens."

Jess patted the dirt in with the shovel and adjusted the fencing over it. "It's nothing. I hope it helps a little to deter whoever is doing this. They'll know someone is even more aware of what they've done. I worry about you and think you should consider a good house alarm system. I'll recommend some if you'd like."

She planted her hands on her hips. "But no one's tried to harm me, like poor Jenny or Malia."

With the cage secured, he turned and met her gaze. "You can't compare yourself to their situation. This is definitely weird. You can't know what you're dealing with for sure."

"All right. I'll think about it."

"Good." He picked up his shovel and tool bag. "I have the late shift today, so I better get going."

"Okay. Thanks again." Lei stepped across the grass, her flip-flops tapping on her heels as she walked toward the kitchen door entrance.

Jess returned home, locked his shovel and tools in the shed and headed inside for a shower. After dressing in his uniform, he had time to check his email before he left for work.

His head jerked forward when a sender caught his eye. An email from Eva Rose.

165

Dear Daddy,

He gasped as his fingers touched his parted lips. Tears welled up in his eyes. He loved Eva Rose so much. Calling him her daddy was a most special gift.

Mom is helping me write this. Thank you for the dress and the toys and books you brought for me. I like them a lot and had a fun time when you came to visit me. I hope you can come and see me again real soon, Daddy.

Love,

Eva Rose

Tears stung his eyes, and he wiped them away. Her words broke his heart. When would he have the funds to afford to visit her again? He missed her so much, and he'd only been home a couple of days.

He'd reply to Eva Rose later on tonight, but wished he could respond to the comment about seeing her again soon.

Jess glanced at the other emails. His eyes widened. One from the company he'd waited for from Oahu. He couldn't help but skim through it and then reread it more carefully. They wanted to interview him on site at Oahu.

His heart skipped a beat and his thoughts scattered. He'd waited so long for this. But how might it affect his life now? Things had changed a lot since he'd applied, especially with Lei and Eva Rose, both so important to him now. What would Lei say since the job might become a reality? He'd have to tell her.

Jess would call the company and set up the interview as soon as he told Lei and head out to work. She wanted and deserved his honesty and he'd deliver.

He all but sprinted across the lawn, through the bushes, and into her yard. Breathless, he rapped on the kitchen door.

The deadbolt unlatched with a click and she opened the door and screen for him to enter.

"Jess. I didn't expect to see you again so soon."

"I know." He rubbed his palms together. "But I got an email, and I thought I should tell you right away."

Brows knit together, she squinted. "What is it?"

Breathless, his pulse rose. "It's from the company on Oahu. They want me to come for an interview."

Her jaw dropped open. "Wow. Congratulations. I know it's what you've wanted for so long. I'm so happy for you."

"I plan to set it up as soon as possible." With his hand on her shoulder, he cleared his throat. "Sorry, it's a lot to dump on you today, but we'll talk later, okay? Time for me to head to the hotel now."

Her voice softened. "I do appreciate you letting me know."

Jess turned and walked back to his house. Lei said she was happy for him, but she didn't say much else. No surprise there. He understood. But what if he received the position and lost her in the process? Was the job worth it? Did she love him enough to consider a future with him if he moved to Oahu? And what was best for Eva Rose concerning this job?

Remaining calm was the best thing for now. If they hired him, he had a little time to make a decision, hopefully the best one for all concerned.

CHAPTER SEVENTEEN

Two days later, steam poured out from the pot of *saimin* as Lei stirred it, while waiting for Malia to arrive for dinner. She put a lid on the pot and turned the burner on low. The soup reminded her of when their mother had made it for them during their early years. Comfort food then and also now.

A sharp rap on the door led her to look out of the small, peephole window. Malia's beautiful smile.

She opened the door and embraced her sister. "Welcome."

"Thanks." Malia stepped inside and glanced around the kitchen. "Each time I come, this plantation house looks cozier than the last."

"I'm trying." She motioned for Malia to sit in a kitchen chair. "I've enjoyed living here."

"Good to hear." Malia's lips formed a thin line. "Except for the strange digging now and then, I'm sure."

"Yeah. It's odd. But no real harm done." Lei seated herself at the table. "I don't think I told you Jess put a wire, fence-like cage around the area this time. It might make it a little harder to dig through there since it's partly attached to the house. We'd like to think someone would get the message to leave it alone, but it's hard to say if they will."

Malia fluffed her hair behind her shoulders. "Jess has been so good to support you, hasn't he?"

"Absolutely. I do appreciate his help." She stepped to the stove and opened the lid on the soup to stir it again.

Malia turned toward her. "You haven't said much about him since he traveled to the mainland. Are you two doing okay?"

"Yes, but he has a lot going on. Besides trying to get to know his daughter and do what's in her best interest, he has a job interview today on Oahu."

Her voice intensified as she gripped the edge of the table. "Is it for the job he has wanted for so long?"

"Yes."

"So they finally contacted him." Malia leaned forward. "What will it mean for you if they offer him employment, and he accepts it?"

Lei planted her hands on her hips, not ready to consider it until he'd informed her of the outcome. "I have no idea." The lid clanked when placed back on the pot, and she returned to the chair. "He needs a job, especially since his time at the hotel is nearing the end. But he has to consider Eva Rose, too. Those are the big decisions he has to make now."

"Wow. It's a lot to consider." Malia stared at her. "I suppose you'll find out soon enough."

"He'll let me know about the interview when he returns later." She rolled her shoulders, hoping to ease the increased tension. "Let's go into the living room until we eat."

Her sister entered the living room, sat on the couch and picked up one of the purses Lei had made to sell. "These are super cute."

"Take one, a small gift for you." Lei sat across from her. "Now tell me how the investigation is going."

"Thanks." Malia tucked a blue and tan purse by her side and cleared her throat. "The mechanic stated the jobs he accepted were presented to him as typewritten messages from someone who dropped them off at his shop with a down payment. Wearing a hood, face partly concealed, the messenger didn't enter a car outside when he left, so no automobiles or license plates were available to check for reference, as stated by the mechanic. And often he'd receive phone calls requesting him to carry out jobs. Once the mechanic completed the requested task, he received the payment in full afterwards, delivered at a designated place."

"Wow. An organized, planned setup to keep things well hidden and to protect them."

"Yeah, they must be quite professional at this." Malia sat upright. "Get this. The mechanic received payment at a post office box and received instructions for what time to pick up his money. They must not have wanted him hanging around or frequenting the post office and getting noticed, the investigator said. But one day the payment wasn't there on time, so the mechanic waited outside near some bushes. He saw a man walk in and exit a few moments later. Then a lady entered. The mechanic went back into the post office a few minutes later and his money was there. He claims he can recognize the man and the lady and is searching through photos of people with police files which fit their descriptions. The police and investigator believe the most recent case of altered brakes reported is linked to my car's damage, with both cars worked on by the mechanic. He should feel some pressure when presented with the information."

"So they're finally getting somewhere with connecting the case with the others." With a lightness in her chest, she rushed to Malia's side and squeezed her shoulder. "The police and investigator should have a strong case soon, I would think. I so want this to be over for you and Jenny's parents."

"Me, too." Malia rubbed her eye. "It'll be some closure for them. The police and investigator both said the guy might turn state's evidence, especially if they find anything more on him. In the meantime, there's enough to warrant a preliminary hearing for the mechanic, considering all the unscrupulous jobs he's taken. I'll let you know as soon as I hear any more information."

"Good. I'll be there for you. Let's go into the kitchen and have something to eat. I want you to get home before it turns dark."

Lei entered the kitchen, filled two bowls with the saimin and placed them next to the chopsticks and ceramic spoons on the table. "The saimin may not be as good as Mom's, but it'll suffice." She pulled out a chair, leaned over and blew across the hot bowl of broth.

The phone vibrated. She checked the caller ID and faced Malia. "It's Jess. Do you mind if I take this?"

"Please, go ahead." Malia scooped more noodles.

She walked away from the table. "Hi, Jess. Are you home?"

"I'm at the Kahului airport. It'll be too late to spend much time and talk with you when I arrive home, so I'll see you tomorrow with all the details. What's up with you?"

What all should she say or ask? "Malia's here for dinner." Her jaw quivered. "How did your day go?"

"Great. Then again, I guess it depends on one's perspective."

Lei squeezed the phone. Her throat tightened. Did he assume she wouldn't agree? Her pitch rose. "Tell me what happened."

"They offered me the job, and I accepted it."

"Congratulations, Jess. I'm so happy for you getting the position you've wanted for so long."

"Thanks, I appreciate it. There's so much I need to share with you and ask you. I'll be over bright and early."

"Okay. Night, Jess." She ended the call and returned to the kitchen.

Malia stared at Lei with a quizzical look. "Everything work out okay?"

She sat on the edge of the kitchen chair and fiddled with the phone. "One of his decisions I mentioned earlier has occurred. He accepted the job offer, which means he will move to Oahu, eventually. I won't know the details until tomorrow. I thought he might go back to the mainland, but since he's out of work at the hotel here soon, he definitely needs a decent paying position. Now he'll have one and it's what he's wanted."

A hint of doubt showed in Malia's eyes before her sister turned away. Her voice softened. "I hope you're prepared for what might come next."

Fidgeting in the chair, her tone increased. "The situation is what it is, Malia, regardless of anyone's concerns or opinions right now."

Preparation for what? Saying good-bye to him for good? Choosing between him and her life here? Of course, it depended if he wanted their relationship to continue now. She didn't know what to think and most certainly wasn't ready to talk about it.

*

Lei rose earlier than usual the next morning and dressed in the blue and lavender floral print sundress she'd wear for work at the hotel later. In the kitchen, she opened the Kona coffee bean container and added some extra beans in the grinder to make it stronger, the way Jess liked it. The aroma of the ground beans smelled so fresh and pungent. The banana bread, oranges and a few pastries on the table finished preparations for his arrival, so she could spend the time focusing on what he had to say.

She recognized his strong rap on the kitchen screen door. "Anybody home?"

"Come on in, Jess." She filled two ceramic mugs with coffee and placed them on the kitchen table.

Jess greeted her with a huge hug. His warmth against her face and his aftershave smelled wonderful. He pulled back and his green eyes sparkled. "Good morning. You look beautiful."

"Thank you." She gazed into his eyes. "Welcome home. I'm so glad to see you." She'd missed him, even if the trip had been a short one.

They sat at their usual places at the table with their coffee at hand. Jess took a sip. "Ah. No one makes coffee as good as you."

She smiled, handed him a napkin and nudged a plate toward him. "Thanks. Have something to eat and tell me everything."

"The job has great benefits and is definitely what I trained for." He buttered some banana bread. "In time, there's room for advancement. I couldn't turn it down, needing the work and a good salary, especially now when I have to consider Eva Rose."

"It sounds perfect for you. And yes, it'll give you the financial security you've sought for Eva Rose, too, and allow you more visits with her."

He raised a brow. "I have to admit you were right about me considering moving to the mainland. I was tempted, but realized this is the best overall decision. It wasn't only about me, and what I desired with Eva Rose, living closer and seeing her more often. But rather about what's best for her overall, as well as good for the other aspects of my life."

Was she one of the other aspects? She took a gulp of coffee and tried to remain calm. "It must have been a difficult decision."

Jess ate the last of the banana bread and took another swig of his coffee. "At first. But after thinking it through, I couldn't turn down the offer. In the meantime, looking for housing and considering all the details for the move to Oahu need completion while I'm here on Maui. Once I'm finished working at the hotel, I'll have a few weeks to finish settling into another place before my new position begins."

"Makes a lot of sense. But you'll have to start looking right away."

"Definitely." He leaned forward. "Will you consider doing something for me?"

With lips pursed, her posture grew rigid. "What is it?"

WHERE SHE BELONGS

"I would like your help in viewing housing there in a few days. You should remember I don't know much about décor, for starters. Two heads are better than one, as the saying goes. It'll help me decide and will also give you the chance to see a bit of Oahu. And give us a little time together, too. It wouldn't hurt for you to get away for a day either, you know."

She lowered her gaze. "Jess, I—"

He interrupted, his words fast and clipped. "Don't say no right now. Please say you'll consider it. I'm not asking anything more of you, okay?"

Was he afraid she'd say no if he asked more of her? She didn't know what to think. Who knew how serious he was concerning her now? "I'll think it over. But I need to check with Malia first. There's a preliminary hearing coming up regarding the case with the mechanic who rigged Malia's car brakes and I told my sister I'd come and support her."

"Of course. It's a good sign for the case." He pushed his chair back from the table. "Let me know as soon as possible. I'm interested in what you'll think of the housing opportunities and remember, I would love to spend a day with you, even if it's partly for business on Oahu."

"I'll call Malia." She grabbed her mug with both hands. "As soon as she has the date of the hearing, I'll let you know."

He stood and tilted his head to the side. "Good. I meant to ask you if you purchased a home security alarm yet."

"I did. They'll let me know when they can install it."

Jess smiled, gave a thumbs up and left. The screen door clattered behind him.

She rose and tapped her nails on the mug. A trip to Oahu wouldn't hurt a bit, would it? Dressed and ready for work now,

175

maybe she'd go in early and give Malia a call before opening for business. She should be awake by then. Likely the hearing wouldn't occur before Jess wanted to go to Oahu.

After she arrived and set up the table with her creations for sale, time permitted a walk into the courtyard. She passed two fragrant, pink plumeria, and a silvery, koa tree before reaching the sidewalk in front of the beach. The fresh, salt air brought in by the trade winds tousled her hair and rippled her dress. Staring out across the water, she viewed Lana'i to the left and Moloka'i across the channel to the right, its mountain peaks shrouded in clouds. And behind it to the left, a much smaller-looking island due to the distance, lay Oahu. So close, but yet so far.

Seated on a bench behind the sidewalk, she made the call. "Hi, Malia. I wanted to check with you on the approximate date of the hearing for the mechanic. Do they have any idea yet when it might take place? Jess wants me to go for a day trip to find housing for him on Oahu a couple of days from now. But I want to make certain I'm available so I can attend the hearing when it begins."

Malia's voice quivered. "I was about to call you."

Eyes closed, Lei rubbed the middle of her forehead. She recognized the familiar anxious tone in Malia's voice. "Don't worry about the date right now. If something's wrong, tell me."

"Wait, I'm checking my daily planner. I made a note about it. My news may take a while."

She took in rapid, shallow breaths. "Okay." Ocean waves washed up into the sand with a roar while she contemplated what happened with Malia.

"The soonest they think a hearing might be scheduled is more than a week away, maybe longer if they don't have all the evidence they want gathered. The date is tentative yet, but it won't be this soon. Go ahead and take your trip. It'll be a nice break, well, from everything."

Her pitch rose. "Tell me what happened."

"I hope you're sitting down, Lei."

"Yes, I am. You're making me nervous."

"I heard from our brother. He said the mechanic identified Kimo as the man he'd recognized at the post office boxes."

"What?" She jolted up from the bench, and her heart hammered. "No."

"It's awful. He swears he didn't have anything to do with it or give anything to the mechanic."

The coffee she'd drank earlier roiled like pure acid into her throat. "I should hope not."

"He'll see an attorney soon and will be present when the mechanic is questioned."

She gasped. "How can he afford a lawyer?"

"Dirk's covering for it until Kimo receives his share of Tutu's money."

"Thank heavens." She blew out a breath.

"Kimo wants to speak with us about the situation, but not until after he meets with the attorney. So take your trip. There's nothing else to do right now with the case."

Her heart pounded. "Are you sure? Would you like me to stay with you? This is shocking."

"No, I'm fine. It'll all get sorted out. And Dirk will support Kimo for now, too. Kimo's adamant he didn't do it. I believe him, but yeah, it was a shock at first. If Kimo had paid the mechanic, it might've connected him to the case, especially if he knew what the payoff entailed. But he didn't, thank heavens. It should turn out okay. Things could be worse, I suppose."

"Yeah. But be sure and let me know if there's anything I can do or if there is any more information in the meantime."

"I will. Thanks. I feel better just having talked with you. Have a pleasant trip."

Pulse racing, Lei wasn't sure what to think. After a few deep breaths, she glanced at her watch and had enough time to call Jess before he left for work. She wanted to take the trip, but prayed she wasn't making a mistake by leaving, if only for a day.

CHAPTER EIGHTEEN

Two days later, Lei sat next to Jess on a Hawaiian Airlines plane headed for Oahu. As they passed the sharp cliffs of Molokai, she drank the orange-passion fruit juice the stewardess had brought. With the cup back on the tray table, she turned away from the window toward Jess. "Everything has such a different perspective from here. It's beautiful."

He took her hand in his. "So you're enjoying your first flight?"

"Yes, it's awesome." The stewardess came through the aisle with a bag to collect their cups. Another look out the window and she recognized Diamond Head as the plane passed over the crater. "Wow. We're here so soon. This flight is brief."

"I'd like for you to come again when you can explore the island. But thanks for coming with me today to help." He squeezed her hand. "Having you here makes it all the more special."

"You're welcome. I think I'm the one who is treated special today." The beautiful string of hotels along the shores of Waikiki Beach came into sight as the plane veered to the right and descended past the high rises of downtown Honolulu. She moved closer to the window. "I see Pearl Harbor below."

Jess nestled his face next to hers. "We're descending more, so look for the Arizona Memorial."

The white oblong structure shone bright in the harbor. With a jolt back, her voice rose. "There it is. It's so cool to see all of this for real, and not just on television or in photos."

Once the plane landed and they entered the airport, the floral smell permeated the air. Jess purchased a white, tuberose lei from a small kiosk and placed it over her shoulders. He gave her a quick peck on each cheek. "Welcome to Oahu."

Lei gazed into his eyes and placed her hands on his shoulders. She wanted the moment to last forever. "Mahalo. Thank you so much for your thoughtfulness. I've never received flowers from anyone."

"I promise you it won't be the last time." His eyes softened with an inner glow, and his knuckles grazed her cheek. "No one deserves them more than you."

They left the airport, connected with the realtor and viewed two condos. The third rental was a small plantation-style cottage house adorned with red ti leaf in front, not unlike the ones they each lived in on Maui. A small yard surrounded the tan, wooden house.

Inside, she couldn't help but be reminded of her own house and the land she loved at home. Thoughts of the brief time living next to Jess surfaced and also the powerful connection to Maui, her mother, Tutu, Malia and Kimo. But this was Oahu.

After they finished surveying the house, Jess turned to her. "What do you think might work best between the three properties?"

She put an index finger to her lips. "This house isn't as modern as the condos and needs a little elbow grease, but it's the only property with two bedrooms and a yard, as small as it is. It's farther from downtown, but it's in more of a suburban area. Not as quiet as where we live, but less hectic than downtown Honolulu, from what I saw. And also, it would be nice for Eva Rose to have a room when she's able to visit as she grows older."

Jess placed his hands on either side of her face. "I was hoping you'd see something good in this property. It has an option to buy, and it's the closest of the three rentals to my job. The prices are all similar and in my range, so no worry there. The suggestions for Eva Rose have me sold."

After Jess made the arrangements for renting the house, they flew home. Nightfall arrived as Jess followed Lei into the plantation house. She switched on the kitchen light. "You didn't have to come in with me. It's been a long day."

"I'll take a quick look out the bedroom window since it's dark out now and we weren't home all day. Looks like the kitchen and living areas are fine. Can't be too careful anywhere these days."

Lei sat in the kitchen chair. He probably didn't want her to focus too much on the trespassing from before, but to pay attention, too. She closed her eyes for a moment. His concern was unending. She'd miss him when he left. He hadn't brought up the subject of their relationship in the future and of course, neither had she.

He returned to the kitchen. "Everything looks fine. Guess I'll go home. We got a lot accomplished today. Thanks so much."

"I'm so glad for you. With a new job and now a residence, you'll soon be all set. I hope your relationship continues to progress with Eva Rose, too. I'm sure she'd love to visit you on Oahu when the time is right."

His eyes widened. "Oh, I forgot to tell you. Her mother is engaged. There's a possibility they might honeymoon in Hawaii and even bring Eva Rose along."

She planted her hands on the table and tipped her head back. "Oh, Jess, how wonderful."

"I know you didn't have the opportunity to get a good feel for Oahu and as I mentioned, I hope you'll make another trip in the future. I know you love it here and so do I, but I hope you'll consider what I asked you a while back, if you could ever consider living anywhere else in the future." He leaned over and kissed her, his warm hands on her cheeks and left for home.

How would life proceed without him? Lei continued to sit at the table, contemplating what he'd said.

Yes, she'd had only a slight taste of Oahu and enjoyed what little she saw, but visiting other places had no impact on her by themselves. The connections to her life on Maui did. Was it more about the people than the place?

Time to dig deep inside herself and consider what Pastor Kane had suggested about dealing with life issues. Then she should answer Jess's question.

Their day together had also given her a lot to think over. Jess had made his decisions concerning where he'd work and live. She couldn't use the excuse for waiting on his decisions any more. So it came down to their relationship.

But for now she'd return to the concerns with Kimo regarding the post office boxes, supporting Malia and the investigation involving the rigged car accident and Jenny's death. And with any luck, no one would trespass into her yard again.

*

Two weeks passed, and the date of the preliminary hearing arrived. Lei sat in the courthouse in Kahului with Malia, Dirk, Kimo and his attorney and continued listening to the proceedings.

A gray-haired older man, Guy Lucas, the mechanic, sat in the witness chair for a cross-examination from a lawyer.

A balding, middle-aged attorney in a blue suit questioned the mechanic. "Mr. Lucas, do you routinely perform uncustomary requests by patrons for pay?"

"Cost of living ain't cheap here. I need the money and I perform what services they request. They're the clients and are the ones who make the requests, not me."

The man wanted to defend himself. Not too surprising.

The attorney's voice rose. "Even if it hinders the vehicle's safe performance?"

Mr. Lucas stared downward. "It's not my business to question what they want or why they want it. Maybe they want to test the car—"

"Answer yes or no, please." The attorney's face grew red.

The mechanic's voice softened. "Well, um, yes."

How evident Mr. Lucas wanted to remove himself from the criminal actions. Hopefully the attorney would gather enough information on Mr. Lucas today to grant a formal hearing, and with luck Mr. Lucas would reveal his sources. With poor Jenny Taylor dead, someone should be brought to justice and held responsible. And the sooner, the better.

The attorney faced Mr. Lucas. "You did indeed cut or alter the brake lines of said vehicles belonging to Evan Hamura and Malia Hudson, correct?"

Lei squeezed Malia's hand. Her sister needed all the support she could find.

Mr. Lucas faced the attorney. "Yes, sir."

Jenny's parents sat near the front and had barely moved a muscle. How difficult it must've been for them to see the man who cut the car brakes which led to their daughter's death.

The attorney turned away from Mr. Lucas. "And you have previously stated you were to pick up your payment in cash at a post office box at a designated time. But payment was late one day, so you waited outside, saw a man and a lady go inside the building. The man left before you entered, correct?"

"Yes. The man left. I went in and my money was there."

The attorney stepped closer to Mr. Lucas. "And you've stated this man made your payment, correct?"

"Yes."

"Is the man present in the courtroom today?" The attorney surveyed those seated in the courtroom.

Lei trembled as she observed Guy Lucas stare at Kimo. She turned toward her brother, who gazed downward.

"Yes. Right there." Mr. Lucas pointed at Kimo.

"Let it be noted Mr. Lucas has pointed out Mr. Kimo Hudson." The attorney stepped toward Mr. Lucas again. "It's important to have the correct facts, wouldn't you say, Mr. Lucas?"

"Yes, sir."

"Tell me, how do you know for certain Mr. Hudson placed the money in the post office box? Did you see him perform this task?"

Mr. Lucas tipped his head to the side. "No. I said I was outside."

"Yes, you did. So it could've been the lady in place of Mr. Hudson, or even someone else inside the premises possibly, correct?"

Guy Lucas stammered. "I didn't think so, but I-I suppose."

"I have no more questions for Mr. Lucas at this time."

The man returned to his seat.

Kimo was called to the stand and sworn in.

Lei blinked back a few tears.

The attorney approached him. "Mr. Hudson, do you recognize the man we've previously identified as Guy Lucas?"

"No, sir, I don't."

The lawyer scratched his chin and turned. "Were you at said postal area at the time he stated in the previous documentation?"

He bit his lip. "Yes, I was. But I don't remember seeing him."

"And what was your business at the post office on the day in question?"

Lei's pulse soared. Her brother was on the witness stand for a hearing revolving around Jenny Taylor's death.

Dirk leaned forward.

Malia placed a hand over her mouth.

Kimo fidgeted with his hands. "I was headed to deliver an envelope in one of the post office boxes."

The attorney tipped his head to the side. "Would it have been for Mr. Lucas?"

"I don't happen to know the name of the recipient." Kimo cleared his throat.

Lei's stomach fluttered, and she squeezed Malia's hand tighter.

Pamela Harstad

"Can you please tell me the number of the box you opened, Mr. Hudson?"

"Yes, of course. It was 816." He glanced in the direction where she, Malia and Dirk sat.

The lawyer raised his head. "Let the record show this is not the box number previously identified where Guy Lucas collects his payment."

Thank goodness. As Lei's shoulders slumped, what little energy she had left dissipated.

Malia let out a sigh.

Once again, the attorney stepped closer to Kimo. "Do you have any recollection of who else was in the post office at the time, particularly a woman?"

"No, sir, I don't. But I normally don't look around or pay attention to who is there."

The attorney faced the bench. "Your Honor, no further questions at this time."

The judge banged his gavel on the desk. "Court will recess for one hour."

Lei faced her sister. "Thank heavens Kimo's innocence shows in a more positive light." She gazed past Malia at Dirk. "I want to thank you for your support today and for hiring an attorney for Kimo."

"Of course." Dirk leaned closer. "We know he didn't do this deed and soon everyone else will, too."

Malia reached out and touched Dirk's forearm. "I hope they do find who is behind all of this soon, but I'm so glad he wasn't identified as the accomplice. I knew he was innocent."

"We all did, Malia. There are cameras around the area, but they don't always show exactly what box someone opens. But it

186

sounds as though the two areas were separated enough." Dirk fidgeted with his tie. "They needed to discredit Guy Lucas's testimony against Kimo, and they did. Box 816 is rented by Kimo's boss, too."

Dirk's information proved thorough, but he'd been privy to more information from Kimo and possibly the attorney. "Thanks, Dirk. You've been a tremendous help." Lei rose and shook his hand.

"I'll tell you what. Why don't the three of you head to my place and visit while I get back to work?" Dirk stood. "I know Kimo wants to talk with you."

After Dirk left, Kimo walked toward them with a smile. Lei hugged him, followed by Malia.

They drove to Dirk's home on the crest of a hill overlooking the Pacific, entered the huge, sunk-in living room and rested on the large sectional sofa.

Kimo folded his hands and sat forward on the edge of the couch. "First of all, thanks for coming. Nerve-wracking doesn't begin to describe how I felt on the stand. I know I haven't been the best brother recently, but you two are the greatest sisters a guy could ask for."

Lei nodded and put her purse at her side. This was the Kimo she once knew.

Malia's voice was soft. "You're our brother. We love you."

"I have something I want to tell you both." He took in a large breath. "I've taken care of it now. It could've come out in court. Please don't get upset."

Lei's chin dropped, her body heavy. "What is it?"

"When I looked for work, Dirk gave me some employment websites to check out. I found one as a courier with some businesses. It paid well enough, and I delivered stuff." He paused. "Lots of it to the same post office box area. It's probably why Guy Lucas recognized me there."

Malia's eyes widened. "If nothing else, it gave you a plausible reason for being at the location, after what we heard today. But what did you deliver?"

He rubbed his palms back and forth. "I don't know and I didn't care until now."

"But you quit the job, right?" Lei's heart fluttered in her chest.

"Yeah, right after I got pulled into this court case. I guess I got scared and didn't stop to think what I was doing might be shady. And after questioning by the attorneys, especially today, it's not fun. Even when you're innocent."

Malia turned toward him. "You did the right thing. And as long as you don't know what kind of dealings they were, it's probably for the best. Another job will come along."

"Malia's right, Kimo. You've done what you can for now. But in time, it might not hurt to check into who these companies are or if they're even legit in case someone tries to connect or blame you for something in the future you didn't have knowledge of, like what happened to you today. If apprehended for something, they would try to put the blame or pressure back onto you to cover themselves."

Malia faced Lei. "I couldn't agree more."

Lei drew in a breath. "What happened to Guy Lucas is a good example. So far, he's the only one facing a trial, not those who hired him. You need to protect yourself as much as possible. Look what happened to Jenny. Or would've happened to Malia from someone who tampered with her car brakes. I think we've all learned things can snowball quite fast from an underhanded situation."

Kimo looked up at her. "Yeah, for sure. Excellent idea."

Malia nodded. "Lei and I will try to help you in any way we can. We'll also continue with the private investigation Jenny's parents have in progress, to help find the culprit in the case. I'll alert them about this, too."

Lei steepled her fingers. "Don't worry, Kimo, we'll help you as best as we can, and also get to the bottom of this case."

"Thanks for understanding. I want to call Elle since she couldn't get off from work today and fill her in about what's happened so far at the hearing." He stood.

When Lei rose to hug him, her purse dropped onto the floor. "Great." She rolled her eyes and picked up what fell on the sofa while Kimo grabbed the rest from the floor and put it in the purse. "Thanks. Now for a hug." She embraced him.

After Malia hugged him, he left the room.

"I'm glad Kimo came to terms with this on his own." She faced Malia. "My concern is if his job deliveries might be called into question and tarnish his reputation or cause him legal problems. Thankfully, he wasn't the one who delivered pay for Mr. Lucas."

Malia stared out the window. "Yeah, but let's hope there's no connection."

Lei jerked back, unbridled energy pumping through her shaky limbs. "What? I don't even want to consider it as a possibility. You said you believed Kimo."

"Yes, but if he doesn't know what he delivered and for whom, it's a little scary. What if those businesses he talked about working for are part of a similar scam?"

"But we do know he didn't deliver anything to Mr. Lucas. Don't go borrowing trouble and making assumptions. It's bad enough as it is."

"You're right. I have to remember it was a different mailbox and it's what matters for now. I'm getting carried away, I guess."

Lei tapped an index finger against her lip. "No, maybe you're right. I didn't want to think such a thing, but it is best to keep all possibilities in mind. It could well be worth pursuing for Kimo's sake, in case. Let's pray this all comes to a head soon."

Malia ran a hand through her hair. "Yeah, it's been hard on everyone."

"I need to head for home." Lei hugged her sister. "Keep me posted on what else happens."

After returning home, Lei entered the house and walked straight into the bedroom. She threw her purse on the vanity and flopped onto the bed.

More at ease about Kimo, she wasn't sure how to approach Jess and their relationship. The lengthy drive hadn't helped bring any decisions to the forefront as for how to answer him. One thing for sure, she had much to pray about tonight. She'd finally learned to give it all up to God. Tomorrow she'd talk to Jess. He deserved an answer.

CHAPTER NINETEEN

At home after a long day at work, Lei picked up the phone from the kitchen counter and headed outside. A cool breeze refreshed her as she walked into the backyard, a reminder fall would usher in subtly and how quickly time passed.

Seated in one of the lawn chairs in the shade, she glanced at the hibiscus bushes toward Jess's house. He would come join her after he returned from work. In the meantime, she'd give Malia a call. The wind blew her hair, and the fallen plumeria danced through the yard while she waited for her sister to pick up the phone.

Malia answered on the third ring, her voice husky. "Hey, Lei."

"You sound out of breath. Did I take you away from something?"

"No, but I did just finish speaking with Jenny's mother."

"Go ahead and fill me in. I'm listening." She pressed the phone closer to her ear.

"You remember the woman at the hearing they spoke about seeing at the post office boxes along with Kimo?"

"Yes, of course." She stared downward, her gaze unfocused.

"Authorities watched for where she made the deliveries, and the investigator has taken photos of her inserting payments into specific postal boxes as well as other deliveries elsewhere. Today, they showed a photo of her making payment in the post office box where Guy Lucas claims he receives his payments."

Her heart triple-hammered. "Whoa."

"He looked mortified on the stand, but wouldn't admit to her possibly making the payment to him. And if he truly doesn't know her, it stands to reason they didn't have a personal, legitimate business deal. The lady has notorious ties to a questionable organization. It sounds like they might hold her fully responsible for paying Mr. Lucas to cut the brakes unless the woman admits someone hired her to deliver the pay. She was obviously at the postal area the day he received pay, too. So they think she'll cooperate, since otherwise she'll likely take the biggest fall for it."

A hand flew over her chest. "Amazing. They've done a lot more investigation than we realized and are getting somewhere with this case now."

"Who knows what they'll come up with before this is over?"

A gaze toward the bushes showed no sign of Jess yet. "One good thing is this new information definitely lets Kimo off the hook for any involvement with Guy Lucas in this case."

"Yeah. But you haven't heard the worst of my news yet."

Her eyes wide, Lei's pitch heightened. "What now?"

"Kimo and Elle had to each pack up their rooms and move out of Dirk's house today. He kicked them out with no warning whatsoever. Kimo said Dirk didn't tell them why he did it, either. I'm letting Elle sleep in Jenny's old room until our new tenant moves in with us and Kimo is on the couch."

Her voice shrill, a coldness hit at her core. "Are you serious?" She lowered her head and squeezed her eyes shut a moment. "It doesn't make any sense. Everything was going so well, or so I thought. And now with Kimo out of work, too, it's even worse. Something bad must've happened between them. You don't throw a person out suddenly for no reason."

"Yeah, I agree. There's more to the story we don't know. What a mess on top of everything else. I guess they couldn't stay with Dirk forever, anyway. But Elle has a job and Kimo's looking."

"Good. I hope he takes whatever decent position he can find. Good luck, Malia. Nice of you to take them in or they'd be on the street. Thanks for filling me in on everything. Jess is stopping by soon."

"Sure. Talk to you tomorrow."

Lei stared at the yard, mind racing at what Malia said about Dirk and Kimo. A shadow fell over the grass and she raised her head. There stood Jess, in a gray T-shirt and blue jeans, striking as ever.

"Penny for your thoughts?"

She extended her arm near the other lawn chair. "Join me. I have lots to tell you. More than a penny's worth, I'm afraid."

With a winning smile, he sat next to her and folded his hands while she brought him up to date on the case and the news about her brother.

"Too bad. But once Kimo finds a job, he'll be okay. It's great news he wasn't involved in the situation with Malia's car. And the case sounds like it might have an end in sight."

Lei pushed the bangs out of her eyes. "Thanks, Jess. You always know what to say to make me feel better." She tapped a fist against her lips. "I meant to tell you the alarm system was installed today and there's another camera mounted for inside viewing, too."

"Good. Glad to hear it. Remember to turn the alarm on when you're gone or you go inside for the night. I'd leave the inside camera on all the time, as you do with the outdoor one."

"I will." She rubbed her palms together. Time to answer his question. "I want to talk to you about my connection to my homeland and my thoughts on it."

"If you're ready." He leaned forward in the chair.

"For a long time I thought the only stability I could count on was my native land here on Maui, particularly when I had no one or any family to depend upon. It sustained me when no one else did. I clung to it, maybe out of desperation, especially when I was younger. Logically I understood the land itself wasn't a true substitute, but it was a comfort when I needed it. It was home, where I belonged, when I didn't have one."

"I can understand that."

Lei cleared her throat. "Then I realized it was similar in a way to others depending on physical things for comfort and to cope with life, like my father's addiction, which didn't work in the long run to cope with his problems. I had to dig deeper inside myself to understand my feelings. I see how I limited myself and my life. Now, I feel more secure and can handle issues better. It took some time. I think you, Pastor Kane and of course, God are all responsible for helping me."

Jess took her palm in his and rubbed the back of her hand with his thumb. "You're a strong person. More than you know. You did what you had to do to get by and survive for a long time. And you're the most special woman I've ever known. I love you so much." He rubbed his eye and sat back in the chair.

She leaned toward his shoulder. "I love you, too. And I can live life more freely, even outside the bounds of Maui, if I choose."

"No one wishes for the best in life for you more than I do, whatever it might be." He put his hands through her hair, alongside her temples and leaned in for a kiss. His soft, warm lips drew ever closer to hers and she laced her arms around his neck, bringing him closer and needing him near.

Pulling back, he framed her jaw with his fingertips and stared into her eyes for the longest moment.

"Jess, would you like to stay for dinner?"

"I would, but I promised Mom I'd call and it's getting late on the mainland. I should shower and take care of a few things in the house, too."

Lei's voice softened. "Okay. Maybe I'll see you tomorrow at work."

"Yeah." He tilted his head. "How about if I come over tomorrow night?"

She raised her head, chin jutting upward. "It's a deal."

After Jess left, she headed inside the house. She couldn't believe the weight lifted from her, a light, free feeling. How wonderful an experience after sharing her thoughts with him.

Lei fried the Spam in the skillet and listened to the crackle as it browned. The rice tasted delicious with it. A favorite local food since childhood. Nice to remember the good memories instead of focusing on the difficult ones so much.

With the dishes cleared away, Lei entered the living room, headed straight to the sewing machine and pulled out some blue and purple floral material. She sat at the machine and flipped on its light, thankful the sewing business turned out so well, including the online business. She could make a decent living with it, wherever she might be, if necessary. Part of God's plans for her? She believed it without a doubt now.

The phone buzzed and vibrated in her pocket. She grabbed it. "Hello."

A heavy breath should've prompted her to check who called, but a voice rang out. "Lei. Dirk here."

His words were slow, deliberate. Would he mention something about Kimo? "Yes, hello, Dirk. What can I do for you?"

"I want my knife back."

Had she understood him correctly? Pulse rising, she stuttered. "I-I don't know what you mean? What knife?"

Dirk's voice boomed. "The one Kimo says he didn't take. I had it in my pocket when I sat on the davenport the morning before the three of you came to my house. He's trying to claim you dumped your purse out and you two grabbed whatever was on the sofa and floor. One of the two of you has it."

A missing knife must have been the dispute between them. Her eye twitched and she rubbed it. "Yes, I knocked my purse over by accident. I'll go and check it right now. It's a large handbag, and everything falls to the bottom, so I might not have noticed it." She hurried into the bedroom and dumped the purse contents on top of the quilt on the bed. Sure enough, she found it. "I see it. It's red and has your initials on it."

"Yes. Given to me by my dad. It's expensive."

Heat rose to her cheeks. Hopefully he believed her. "Of course. I'm so sorry and honestly didn't know it had mistakenly gotten shoved in there. In such a hurry, I should've been more careful. Please accept my apology. I'll return it to your house in Kahului tomorrow as soon as possible after work."

"No, it won't work for me. I'll come and get it tomorrow night. I'm traveling toward your direction anyway."

Not the time to argue with Dirk. She'd respect his wishes. "Okay. I'll be here."

The call clicked off.

Dirk's usual demeanor had disappeared. Did he think she'd stolen the knife? It sure sounded like it. Or did he think Kimo stole it, stashed it in her purse, and it's why he told Kimo to leave? A definite possibility. She wouldn't bring up any mention of her brother with Dirk, unless he did. Or maybe Dirk was standoffish since he'd asked Kimo to leave, and she was his sister. Regardless, she hoped he'd cool down by tomorrow night when he reclaimed the knife, but had a strange feeling something else bothered him.

*

The next evening after an early dinner, Lei rested on the sofa with legs curled up beneath her. A glance at the wall clock showed the time as six o'clock. When would Dirk arrive? Best to be ready for him.

She returned to the kitchen and placed Dirk's knife in a paper bag. She turned off the alarm system and left the screen door open since it was light out and expected company.

Jess would stop over, too. He'd be glad to know she remembered to turn the alarm system on before retiring last night and kept it on until returning home today with the indoor camera on, as he'd suggested. The care and compassion he showed her never ended. What did she ever do without him?

The phone rang and she hurried into the living room to answer it. "Hi, Malia."

"I thought I'd fill you in on what I found out today from Jenny's parents after they talked with the investigator."

Back on the sofa, she pressed the phone to her ear. "Wow. More information. They've really moved ahead on things with the investigator, haven't they? Okay. Let's have it."

"They have a connection with a person responsible for hiring the lady to pay Mr. Lucas. There's a phony business with the intent to hide who's behind this. It sounds like a matter of time before the case is solved and they know the truth."

Her shoulders dropped. "Oh, thank heavens. What a relief, not only for Jenny's parents, but for you, too."

"Yeah. I'll feel much better. Less nervous, for sure. Talk to you soon."

"Okay, Malia. Get a good night's sleep for a change."

A car pulled into the driveway. Dirk's green Jaguar.

Her pulse soaring, she hurried into the kitchen. The car door slammed, and she held the screen door open for him to enter.

"Come in, Dirk."

He scanned the kitchen before he stepped into it. "It's the first time I've been invited inside this plantation house. My dad and I spent a lot of time here years ago. Our special place to come and go as we pleased, with no invitations necessary."

Lei extended a palm toward the kitchen table and chairs. "It's great to have good family memories, isn't it?"

"It certainly beats the bad ones." He continued to stand.

"Here's the knife." She picked up the sack and handed it to him. "Again, I sincerely apologize for the mistake and the inconvenience. I should check through my purse more often and watch what I'm doing. My error, totally."

The paper bag crinkled as Dirk pulled the knife from it. He turned it back and forth in his grip, as if to check for damage.

"It should be all right since it sat in my purse without any use." She rubbed her palms together.

His expression grew more serious. "So you keep saying."

Dirk must've thought she'd stolen the knife. Her heart hammered. What else did he want? What was he waiting for? "Can I offer you something to drink?"

He stared at her. "I can help myself."

What did he mean? Was he crazy? She inched back from him. A prickly sensation ran up the back of her neck. "I don't mean to hurry you, but I have company coming soon."

"Yeah, right. Well, this won't take long. I suddenly need a little capital." He flicked up one of the blades of the knife.

Her body tremored. "Dirk, what are you doing? Please put the knife down. I think you should leave."

"Not so fast." He moved toward her. "Let's take a trip into the bedroom. You first."

Her legs weakened as she stepped into the room. Dirk followed her and edged her near the bedroom window. She stood there stone-faced, shaking.

"Stay there." He knelt down and sliced the worn vinyl floor with the knife.

Light-headed, Lei stood rigid and her breathing suspended for a moment. Was he going to do something to her? Put her underneath the floor?

Dirk glared at her. "What's the matter? Not enjoying my family's plantation house like you have been?"

Breathless, her chin quivered. "I-I don't understand this. What are you doing?"

Dirk tugged at the large, vinyl strip he'd cut and it ripped wide open, exposing the subfloor. He pulled at a square wooden lid with a small knob in the middle. It rumbled until it broke loose and he dropped it on the floor at his side. "Let me explain. After my grandfather died, Henry leeched a lot of money from my dad. To make matters worse, Henry married your grandmother and now you three peasants have everything of ours."

She stammered. "But you-you never said you were unhappy about anything, even at the reading of the will."

"Don't insult me." His voice roared. "I'm not stupid enough to say I should've been named executor in the last will and deserved all of Henry's resources in public at an attorney's office."

"You're making assumptions. No one knew if Tutu had you named in the previous will either."

He cocked his head to the side. "You could have had it checked out if you would have cared enough to do it, but does it matter? It was all rightly mine anyway. Being executor would've made it easier, but no, you had to mess it up for me. I offered to help you with the will but you declined, so this is what you get for cutting me out. You should have never had a dime when your grandmother was alive, since the money came from the Carrington family. Henry's so-called wishes to include you didn't override the fact my dad and later on I should have had the money and this house."

Lei couldn't believe the words came out of Dirk's mouth. Who was he? "But you were always friendly around us and—"

Dirk narrowed his eyes with an intense focus. "I kept all of you close at hand thinking I would get what was mine until one of you three somehow made your grandmother change the will. And that brother of yours ended up useless to me, since the idiot quit the job I set up for him and did me no good. And he might've also gotten a payoff if he'd found the ancient fishhooks here. But he couldn't even do a simple task, worthless chump. I would have dangled a few bucks in front of him and the fishhooks would've been mine since I have a right to them, too." He shoved the lid farther away. "Not to mention your sister's interference with him, trying to sway him into what she thought was righteous for him. Sickening. Can't send a boy to do a man's job."

Her eyes bulged as she stared out the bedroom window near the burrowing right behind them. The digging. He wanted something here. Now it made sense. "So you were the one who came and dug around outside."

He smirked. "Not me, you fool. There are people for those tasks." He pulled a steel box from under the opening where he'd pulled off the lid. "But I've got the fishhooks now. They used to be under the lava bed outside. I forgot about this trap door."

Waves of nausea overcame her. She gagged. "Take them and get out of here."

Dirk stood with the knife in one hand and the box in the other. "It's what I intend to do, thanks to you three idiots. I heard what you said at my house. Why do you think I offered to let you use my house to talk?" He backed his way into the kitchen and motioned for her to follow him.

Acid burned her throat, and she covered her mouth. Tears fell. "But you hired an attorney for Kimo and now—"

"You're really dense. I made sure I'd know what was happening. Then you and your sister snooped into stuff which was none of your business and suggested an investigator. You'll all pay for it someday. Malia wouldn't take the hint to get out of the way, and neither did you when you lived in Kahului. I got rid of you before you came to Lahaina, but you took my plantation house and made it worse for me." He held the knife up and the blade looked sharp.

Her mind raced and her eyes bulged, unable to blink. "You were the one who broke my apartment window in Kahului?"

His eyes pierced into her like two daggers. "No, you dim wit. You're insulting my intelligence again. Do you want me to use this knife?"

Afraid to speak again, she shook her head. Her body tremored.

"Don't think you're going to call the cops or threaten me any further. I'm going where no one can find me. Move over here closer to the kitchen table where I can see you." He turned to leave.

Jess stood in the doorway and blocked Dirk.

He pointed the knife at Jess's throat and dropped the metal box on the table with a clank. "What do you think you're doing? Get in this kitchen and get out of my way."

"Fine." Jess raised his hands in the air and stepped inside away from the door. "Take it easy, man."

"Shut up!" Dirk stuck the point of the blade near Jess's throat again, grabbed the metal box and shoved it into Jess's abdomen.

Jess grabbed the box, bent over from the blow and a drop of blood trickled from his neck.

Lei stumbled into the table as she tried to reach Jess and let out a primal scream.

Jess shoved the box back at Dirk, who lost control of the knife and it flung toward Jess. As Jess covered his face with his arm, the knife slit his forearm and clanked onto the counter. Dirk lost his balance, hit his head against the wall and slid to the floor, moaning.

With a dishtowel in hand, she ran to Jess and wrapped his arm to stop the bleeding. "I'm so sorry, Jess."

"Let me get the knife before Dirk does." He hobbled to the counter next to the sink and grabbed it. "We need to get out of here now."

Lei shook as Jess pulled her through the bushes and into his yard.

"You okay, Lei?"

She stuttered. "I-I guess so."

They entered his house. Jess locked the door and peered out the window.

"Shouldn't we call the police?" Lei gasped for air.

He glanced back at her. "I called them before I came to your house. And I got Dirk's license plate number, too."

A car door slammed and an engine roared. Dirk's jaguar squealed out of the driveway in a trail of dust and tore off down the street.

"He's gone." Jess squeezed her shoulder.

"Dirk has to be caught. He talked crazy, like he was running away."

Jess unwrapped the towel and checked his arm. The bleeding hadn't quite stopped, so he covered it a little tighter. "I'll alert the police which direction he's headed." He made the call.

Lei took in some deep breaths while he spoke on the phone, but her heartbeat continued to roar through her ears.

Taking a seat on the sofa, Jess ended the call.

Seated next to him, she stared into his eyes. "Hopefully they'll find him before his planned getaway. How did you know to call them before you came to my house?"

"I walked outside and heard him from over here, with such a loud voice. It's when I came closer, got his plate number and called the police."

She placed a finger near the dried blood on Jess's neck. "You shouldn't have come to my door. Look what happened to you."

"Are you kidding?" He took her hand in his. "I wouldn't have left him with you in the house a second longer."

Lei rested her head on his shoulder and hot tears fell on her cheeks. Tears for his sacrifice, for her safety and for Malia and Kimo. "I can never thank you enough. The three of us siblings foolishly fell into Dirk's clutches. If only we hadn't."

"Shh." Jess brushed the bangs from her eyes. "You couldn't have known, and you're in no way responsible for his actions." He jerked his head back. "I just had a thought. Remember what I told you when I first moved here? I saw the back of a man from a distance walk through the yard before you moved into the plantation house. I didn't see his face or see him for long, but now I wonder if it might've been Dirk. We'll never know for sure, but considering how he planned this whole crazy setup, I wouldn't be surprised."

"Yeah, who would have imagined his elaborate plan." She gazed into his eyes. "Jess, I have to tell Kimo and Malia."

"Yes." He pulled her closer. "Do you want to stay with Mrs. Chen tonight or will you be okay in the house with the alarm system on?"

She turned away from him and lowered her head. "I'll stay in the house. The police are coming."

CHAPTER TWENTY

The next afternoon, Kimo and Malia sat on Lei's sofa after viewing the camera feed of Dirk's actions from last night.

Kimo stared ahead, his gaze unfocused.

Malia's jaw hung open.

Lei had shielded her eyes from part of the video. Even listening again made her jittery and uncomfortable.

She moved forward in the chair and faced her siblings. "I told you it was unpleasant. I have a hard time with it yet, even after I reviewed it with the police and with Jess. It's like a terrible nightmare which probably won't go away for a long time. Dirk wanted me to be sure I knew what he thought of us and why he did this."

"He acted like a different person. It's unbelievable we thought him so kind." Malia wiped an eye. "You'd think we would've caught on to something about him. I feel awful now."

Listening to them broke her heart. "It's what I said to Jess, but he says Dirk's actions are not anyone else's fault but his own." If only she could make herself believe it. Jess not only kept her from harm last night, but he also fought off Dirk. What if his injuries had been more severe? She would have never forgiven herself. "But I must say, I never in my wildest dreams imagined he was behind the mischief at my old apartment. And I never would've related it to all the other things he did either. In my gut, I never thought Eric did it, yet he was the only one causing annoyance at the time. I can't wrap my head around Dirk's actions even now."

Kimo glanced at Lei. "How do you think I feel? Dirk took me in, helped me find work. The job paid well, and I needed the money. Look where it might've ended up for me. I was foolish enough to think he had a good heart and cared." He jerked his chin upward. "Yeah, right. I fell head first into his hands. I let him use me, all in the name of power, control and money. For him. I should've known it was all too good to be true, but all I could see were the benefits I was getting."

"All those times I came to visit Kimo and the things I said about Dirk leading Kimo to a questionable job and disagreeing with him living there were all recorded. Who knows what all I said?" Malia lowered her head. "Dirk never said much to me and maybe the recordings at his home tell why he didn't. He obviously couldn't stand me. But I'm fortunate I wasn't as affected as the both of you. I'm so sorry."

Lei folded her hands to keep them calm. "We're all sorry, Malia. I think it's part of why Dirk was so full of blame toward us, to make us feel guilty and foolish. I guess it's another lesson learned. We need to appreciate the good and helpful people in our lives even more and thank God for getting us through this."

Malia glanced at Lei. "Yeah, it's a better way to look at it."

Lei wouldn't have made such a statement not so long ago. She would've retreated from people. Now, she couldn't help but be thankful of this newfound awareness. God had also worked through Pastor Kane and Jess to help her understand stronger faith from God's love provided what she needed to get through this ordeal.

Lei rubbed her palms back and forth. "For me, I think I've finally learned a few difficult lessons, like not focusing on our past troubles and on what we don't have. But we can learn, move on and help someone else rather than retreating from our hurts or problems."

"Yeah, I suppose it is better than dwelling on it." Kimo stood.

Lei tucked a wisp of hair behind her ear. "Kimo, do you want some of the makaʻu when the police return them?"

"No, they're rightfully yours." He stared toward the floor. "I got all wrapped up about them when Dirk first mentioned them. I don't care about them, personally. Besides, I'll have money from Tutu's estate soon enough."

She followed him to the kitchen door and hugged him. "Take care, Kimo."

When she returned to the living room, Malia had taken a phone call.

Seated across from her, she waited until her sister finished the call.

"Jenny's mother called." Malia gazed at her. "The investigator and authorities have the link they need to the business who hired the lady involved and paid Mr. Lucas. They have enough evidence to make charges. We'll know soon. She'll call me later."

Lei rushed to Malia's side and hugged her. "I'm glad we have some good news today. I know we can't bring Jenny back, but I hope you and Jenny's parents can find some peace in time."

"Me, too. When I hear more, I'll let you know."

*

Later in the evening after dinner, Jess put away the last of the dishes into the cupboards and waited for Lei to arrive at his house. He'd worked late, but wanted to spend time with her and see how she'd coped. If she was doing okay, he had some important news to share.

He headed toward the living room when a knock on the door caught his attention. "Come in."

Wearing a white T-shirt and navy capris, hair hanging loose in front of her shoulders, Lei looked gorgeous. No one would've dreamed what she'd been through in the last twenty-four hours.

Lei placed the keys on the kitchen tapa tablecloth she'd made for him. "Sorry if I'm a little late. The police stopped by with the makaʻu they retrieved from Dirk. He'd chartered a plane from the West Maui Airport at Kapalua to take him to a fairly remote outer island, but he never made it. Luckily you alerted the police when you did. Knowing Dirk, he had more plans to move on from there."

"It couldn't have been easy for you, along with everything else you've gone through." Jess walked toward Lei and squeezed her hand. He led her to the sofa and they sat side by side.

"When I looked at all of the makaʻu, I kept thinking of the trauma from Dirk we experienced over them. And for what?" She pushed her hair behind her shoulders.

"They symbolized the money, power and control he wanted or thought was his. What will you do with them?"

209

"Do you think someone who knows about such things would be interested in them?"

"Sure. Possibly a museum curator."

"They truly belong to the people of Hawaii. They're part of its past and future." She moved closer to him.

"The Bishop Museum on Oahu might be a suitable place to start."

She glanced at the bandage on Jess's forearm. "Was the cut deep?"

He raised his arm. "Not too bad. It'll heal in time."

"Good, thank heavens." She moved an index finger near the small nick on his throat from the knife.

He took her in his arms and pulled her close to him. "Everything will work out now."

"Yeah, you're right." She raised her head. "I talked with Malia earlier, and she said they have evidence in Jenny's case. She's supposed to call me back. I'd like to see the case resolved for Malia and Jenny's parents, too. It would be nice to have things settle down around here for a while."

"Yeah. I would think it's a matter of time." Should he tell her the news? He pulled back and searched her beautiful eyes. "I have something to share with you if you're up to it."

Lei's chin lifted. "Of course. It'll be good to have something else on my mind."

Jess drew in a breath and took her by the shoulders. "Eva Rose's mother, Paula and her fiancé Michael, are coming to Hawaii next month for certain. They'll get married and have their honeymoon here." His voice grew louder. "And they're bringing Eva Rose along with them. She and I have bonded quite well and Paula is comfortable with how Eva Rose is handling our relationship as well as with Michael now. So my little girl will stay with me part of the time they are here. My mom's coming to stay a while next month, too. She'll help with Eva Rose. They'll share my room, and I'll sleep on the couch. I can't wait for them to come and for you to meet them."

Palms pressed against her cheeks, her voice sang out. "Wow. How wonderful. Splendid news. And you've got it all planned out, too. I'm so happy for you."

"I didn't think I'd get to see her until next year. And if this visit goes well, Eva Rose might come and stay for a while in the summer next year. It's what I'm hoping for, anyway. I'll have the two-bedroom house then."

"Oh, Jess, it's awesome." She embraced him.

The scent of her hair added to the heat radiating in his chest. He closed his eyes and relished in the feel of her arms around him. "Yes, it is. And so are you."

"It'll be a busy time for you."

Jess turned and glanced at the calendar on the wall. "They'll be here while I'm in this house, but shortly after they leave, I'll head for my new position on Oahu at the end of next month. I don't have much stuff, but I'll start packing what I don't need to use daily as soon as I can."

"I hadn't realized how fast the time has gone." Lei's arms dropped from his neck.

He placed his index finger under her chin and lifted it. "Yes, but you've been a tad busy, which brings me to my next question. I want to discuss something important with you, and I want us to have an evening out somewhere alone together without interruptions. I think we deserve it."

Two fingers touched her parted lips. "All right, Jess." The phone buzzed and she glanced toward her pocket.

"Go ahead and answer it."

Pulling the phone from her pocket, she glanced at the screen and then stared at him. "It's Malia."

Jess moved to the side to give her space.

Lei's voice cracked. "Hello, Malia, I'm listening." She jerked her head to the side. "Are you kidding? What horrible news." She glanced back and forth. "Do you want me to come and stay with you tonight?"

Jess sat upright and rubbed his palms together. What could be so terribly wrong?

"Oh, I forgot you have Kimo and Elle there. Okay. I'll talk with you tomorrow." With the call ended, she wiped her eyes and faced Jess. "They've found out who was behind the entire phony scam business. Dirk's so-called con business hired the mechanic to sever the brakes on Malia's car, obviously meant to hurt or kill her rather than Jenny. It's terribly hard for Malia, since Jenny paid the price and we all knew Dirk, or thought we did."

"Mind blowing." She spoke the sad truth. Jess caressed her shoulder. "No wonder he tried to hightail it out of here in a hurry. He realized it was a matter of time before he faced his horrific actions. Rest assured, his incarceration will last a long time considering Jenny's death, the incident at your house with the ma'kua and his illegal business dealings. Probably a lot more, too."

Jess held her close as she cried. Her needs came first. He'd wait until she was ready, however long it took to have his conversation with her.

*

212

A week later, Lei and Jess pulled into his driveway after a luscious seafood dinner.

With the engine stopped, the dust settled and she opened the car door. "Thanks for a wonderful evening, Jess. I enjoyed every minute of it."

"Wait." He squeezed her forearm. "The most important part of the night isn't over yet."

She tilted her head to the side. "What do you mean?"

"Hold on. You'll see. Follow me." He opened his door. "Okay."

She followed Jess across the street and through the passage of the lava rock wall to the beach. The calm ocean waves reflected the light of the moon, crystal clear tonight. He took off his shoes.

Lei removed her sandals. The sand shifted between her toes and a light breeze blew her hair. "What is it, Jess?"

He faced her and took her hands in his. "It's peaceful here. I wanted such an atmosphere for us to be alone together and to be somewhere near where we first met as neighbors. But not at your house, or my house. Right here by the land and sea. I know they're special to you."

Had something changed? His mother's or Eva Rose's stay? His job? "Yes, we've had many nice evenings here. But is everything all right?"

Jess squeezed her hands. "I hope so. I'll know in a few minutes."

If there was another problem or crisis, she'd scream. "What is it?"

He let loose of one of her hands and kneeled. "I love you with all of my heart. Would you do me the honor of becoming my wife?"

She trembled and a hand came over her lips. "Oh, Jess. I love you so much. I can't believe this. I thought something was wrong. Yes, of course I'll marry you."

"The only problem for me would've been if you turned down my proposal. Right now, I'm soaring sky high." He stood, pulled a box from his pocket and opened it.

The solitaire diamond ring sparkled in the moonlight. "It's exquisite."

Jess slid the ring on her finger. "You've made me so happy."

As a wave crept over the sand, tears slid down her cheeks. "Me, too. It's like a dream I never imagined would come true."

With his index finger under her chin, he lifted her face toward his. "We've come a long way and we belong together."

She loved the sound of his words. "Yes, we do."

"And now we have a wedding to plan. It would be ideal to marry by the end of next month before I have to move and while Mom and Eva Rose are here. But I understand if it's not a long enough time to prepare. I want you to have the kind of wedding you want and deserve."

"I'm not one for large, fancy events. A simple wedding at the gazebo at the hotel would be perfect." She threw her arms around his neck.

Jess pulled her close, kissed her and she was lost in him, a part of him, and belonged with him.

*

214

WHERE SHE BELONGS

The weeks passed by in a hurry, while Lei planned the wedding in time for Jess's mother, Audrey and Eva Rose to attend it today. Dressed in the simple wedding gown she'd made, she gazed in the dresser mirror in the bedroom. The white, floor-length sleeveless A-line dress fit her as she'd hoped.

A rap on the kitchen screen door. "Guess who?" Mrs. Chen's voice.

"My personal attendant? Come in. I'm in the bedroom, Mrs. Chen."

Her flip-flops tapped on the kitchen floor as she made her way into the room. When Lei turned, Mrs. Chen stood in the doorway, hands over her mouth. "Oh, my. So beautiful. I might cry before the wedding, not during it."

She stepped over to Mrs. Chen and hugged her special friend. "We'll both be in trouble if you do."

"Then let's get to work." Mrs. Chen removed the small, white basket from her arm. "Here are some plumeria blooms from my yard for Eva Rose to use as flower girl."

"Thank you. I'll set them on the bed next to the dress I made for her." She never tired of their fresh, floral scent.

Mrs. Chen removed the *haku* lei from her other arm and held it in front of Lei. "Let me put it on you."

She lowered her head while Mrs. Chen placed the floral, wreath-like headpiece in position. A glance in the mirror made her smile. "It's perfect."

The older woman pulled out a lei of tiny, Niʻihau shells from her pocket. "Mr. Chen gave these to me. Now you have something old and borrowed. Your dress is new." She dug into the other pocket. "And a small, blue handkerchief, too."

Warmth filled her. "Oh, Mrs. Chen. How kind of you to offer something so precious of yours to lend me to wear. It means a lot. I don't think I've mentioned this before, but besides appreciating your friendship, it's been like having a mother. Both Jess and I will miss you so much."

"I'll miss both of you, too." Mrs. Chen shook a finger at her. "I'm glad you're keeping this house. You better come back often."

She rested a hand on Mrs. Chen's shoulder. "As often as we can, I promise. And I'll call you, too."

Mrs. Chen's brown, leathered hands came across Lei's cheeks. "I'll be here for you." She took a step back toward the kitchen. "See you at the hotel."

Lei blew her a kiss and waved.

"Knock, knock." She recognized Audrey's voice.

"Come into the bedroom."

Audrey entered the room, her brown hair styled with soft waves. She wore a pale green suit which brought out her green eyes, the same shade as Jess's.

"Welcome, Audrey. Where's Eva Rose?"

The little girl jumped out from behind Audrey and giggled.

Lei opened her arms and reached out to hug the child. "There you are. I'm so glad you're here with us today. Your dress is on the bed. Grandma can help you get ready."

"It's sure pretty." Eva Rose stared at it.

Audrey came closer. "You're absolutely beautiful. I'm so glad you're marrying my son."

What a wonderful thing to say. Her voice softened, and she blinked back tears. "He's the love of my life."

Eva Rose grabbed Audrey's skirt and tugged. "Now I'll have two mommies and two daddies and I have a grandma, too."

Audrey smoothed Eva Rose's hair. "You sure do. I love being your grandma." She turned to Lei. "I want to tell you before the wedding so I won't forget. Welcome. You're a part of our family now."

Lei hugged Audrey. "You don't know what it means to me. Thank you so much. Once Jess and I are settled, we hope to come visit you and Eva Rose. We can't wait."

With final preparations complete, they drove to the Hawaiian Hotel. As Lei stepped into the lobby and remembered her first visit here with Jess, she never would've imagined having her own wedding with him in the courtyard.

Audrey held Eva Rose's hand. "I'm taking Eva Rose over to Mrs. Chen." She bent down towards the girl. "Mrs. Chen will tell you when to walk down the aisle and spread your flowers along the way until you arrive with the rest of the wedding party, where your dad will be standing."

Eva Rose nodded.

Audrey led her away.

Malia came in, hugged Lei and handed her the white, mixed floral, bouquet. "I'm so happy for you. Are you ready?"

She smiled at Malia. "I definitely am, without a doubt."

Her mind drifted to Jeremiah 29:11. *For I know the plans I have for you, declares the Lord, plans to prosper you and not to harm you, plans to give you hope and a future.* The verse had extra special meaning for her now.

After Eva Rose spread plumeria along the way as she walked to the gazebo, Malia paced to the gazebo altar as maid of honor.

Eva Rose grinned up at Jess, whose childhood friend from Oahu stood next to him as his best man.

Pastor Kane smiled at Lei.

Kimo held out his arm for her. "You're beautiful. I couldn't be happier for you."

"Thanks. It means a lot to have you walk me down the aisle."

She took his arm and Kimo walked her along the pathway and left her by Jess's side.

Jess beamed at her and his eyes glistened as the *maile* leaf lei draped around his neck fluttered in the breeze. He took her hand in his and gazed into her eyes. "I'm the luckiest guy in the world. I can't wait to start our life. We're so right for each other."

"Oh, Jess. I love you so much. Yes, we belong together."

As the Hawaiian sun shone down upon them, the ocean waves serenaded them as they recited their vows and became one.

Dear Reader,

I hope you enjoyed reading *WHERE SHE BELONGS* as much as I did writing it. If so, please visit my website listed below for the book's FREE prequel novella, *LEILANI'S STORY*.

Also, a helpful thing you can do is to give an honest review on the Amazon link below by clicking on the book, which can be beneficial for other readers who may enjoy the book.

Please follow me on my Facebook page, Amazon, website and blog listed below for future information about my books. I love hearing from readers!

Thank you,

Pamela Harstad

https://amazon.com/author/pamelaharstad

www.facebook.com/harstadpamela

https://pamelaharstad.wordpress.com

ABOUT THE AUTHOR

Pam enjoys writing contemporary inspirational romance and romantic suspense with emotional themes full of hope and healing in various settings. Her other books include *Erin's Mission, Healing Journey, Their Greek Key* and *As We Forgive Those*. She is a member of American Christian Fiction Writers and is a certified spiritual director. When not writing, Pam enjoys traveling, nature and reading. She lives with her husband in Iowa.

Made in the USA
Monee, IL
15 August 2020

38029992R00135